Children of the Fountain

by
Richard P. Murphy

©2013 Richard Paul Murphy

All rights reserved. This book or any portion thereof may not be reproduced or used in any manner whatsoever without the express written permission of the author except for the use of brief quotations in a book review.

All characters appearing in this work are fictitious. Any resemblance to real persons, living or dead, is purely coincidental.

For more information visit
www.richardpmurphy.com

For Yvonne. I wish you could have read it.

Prologue

The shadow slipped silently through the halls of the abbey. Occasionally, the white of an eye or tooth caught the flickering torchlight. As the figure continued down the main hall, past the kitchens and storerooms it came to a large wooden iron studded door at the end. Slowly, it crept inside, the huge slab of oak seeming to make little protest as it was eased open.

Suddenly the figure froze, and every inch of its body at once became part of the wall; seemingly flatter, almost lifeless. Indeed, the two friars who went past conversing about morning prayers didn't even notice it.

Eventually, the dark shadow peeled itself away from the cloister wall and continued on its course. Never pausing to get its bearings it clearly knew where it was headed.

Turning a final corner it came into a small stone room and the light from a single candle revealed the figure to be that of a man. A bed, desk and some book laden shelves were the only objects present. Sat at the desk a monk scribed away with a quill and parchment, oblivious to the watcher at the doorway. Or so he thought.

"I knew you'd come here eventually. It's been over a year now," said the monk, his eyes barely looking up from the parchment he was decorating.

"Very good, James," came the reply. "You would have made a fine member of the Guard."

"Except I chose another path, father."

Hernan stepped into the candlelight and his lean face was lit instantly. He had been blessed with looks once, but the old features held a darkness also. Pain perhaps? Some past suffering, definitely.

He stepped forward and said, "Whereas my path chose me."

James gave a scoff and stood up; he was younger but his body not as athletic due to his service to God, and wine. Their features were similar but the face of the monk carried no pain or darkness. The eyes glistened even in the candlelight and his smile seemingly warmed the cold the abbey room.

"If you say so, father." James gestured to the seat but the other man remained standing. "You always thought I, rather than Michael, was best suited to your particular line of - "

"I don't have much time. I need you to do something."

"Anything."

"Come with me, I have a carriage outside. I need you to take care of some things."

James followed to the corridor and was nearly too slow to see his father dart through a back door. Emerging in the twilight he almost didn't notice the black carriage discreetly parked beside the copse. Hernan was already there and opening the door when James finally caught him.

"Where are we going?"

"Nowhere," he said, turning with two bundles. "I need you to take care of Michael's children."

"Children! What children?"

Hernan handed over two heaps of rags, which turned out to contain two babies. The monk struggled with them awkwardly, "My God!"

"Margaret gave birth to twins four weeks ago. This is Matthias." Hernan tenderly brushed back the boy's hair as he spoke before continuing, "This here, is Rebecca."

"Where are Michael and Margaret?"

"Margaret is dead, Michael is in hiding."

James stared in shock first at his father and then at the small bundles presented to him. He looked at the boy and saw the small, delicate face was asleep. A sprout of golden hair poked out from a linen cap and the soft delicate lips were unmistakeably his father's. Immediately he imagined the boy's mother staring into those eyes too and spotting the similarities. James clutched the child to his chest and tears fell freely from his cheeks as he thought of Margaret.

"What has happened? Why are they doing this?"

"Michael was right all along. They suspected he knew and tried to kill him. They got Margaret instead, the details of which I'll spare you. I have mourned for her in these brief few hours and I will do so again. But for now, I must see the children are safe. Let's go inside."

They returned to the monk's study and laid the two babies down on a pew.

"James, Michael wants you to look after the children, here, at the orphanage. He wants them to have a different life. I'm sure you of all people can understand this."

James looked at his father and a painful realisation glazed in his eyes.

"You approve?"

"I don't want to put him them in danger. If the Legion ever found out who these children were they may try to complete the circle by killing them."

Hernan walked over to the shelf of books and manuscripts. He idly picked up a small wooden figure of a fox. It was clumsily made, clearly by no craftsman, and the face and features could have been carved by a child. The wood felt rough and chipped in places, sharp edges sat alongside smoothed curves.

"You made this for me?"

"Yes, when I was a boy," whispered James. "Where will you go?"

"Back to the castle, initially. I must check on our latest recruits."

Hernan's head hung low as he held the wooden fox in his hands, his fingers going over every nook and cranny as if he had just finished turning the wood and was inspecting it for mistakes. There were mistakes; too many. "I have to leave," he said.

"After the castle, then what? An attack?"

"No, not yet. I'm leaving for France. England has too many eyes and ears."

"This man, Bonaparte?"

"Nothing to do with us, but we'll keep an eye on him." He turned, placed the wooden carving back on the shelf.

"Goodbye James. One day I hope to return. But for now, bring them up as well as you can. Let them know their father was a good man, a simple man. A farmer, perhaps?"

Hernan turned and went to walk out of the room, his cloak already making him almost invisible in the candlelight. "See to it James. I know you will do what is right. Farewell."

"Tell Michael I will not fail him."

James blinked back tears and when his vision was no longer blurred his father was simply not there. He walked over to the two babies. More tears fell onto the children's cheeks and James wiped them back.

Chapter 1

It was spring and all over Europe men were returning home. A war had been won and slowly the survivors trickled back. From Quatre Bras, Wavre and Waterloo they returned. But here, all those events had passed by like leaves in a stream.

Matthias looked up from the whispering canopy of the orchard. Saint Gregory's Abbey was a run down but happy place to live. True, life was hard in the orphanage. Chores ranged from chopping and collecting wood in the forest for the boys, to hours spent seaming and darning all manner of garments for the girls. But they were happy times for the children who, often, had left behind them great sadness. In each set of eyes there was a different tale of loss; each face covered a miserable truth with smiles and laughter.

A brisk breeze had arrived swiftly that day. Leaves swirled around the courtyard of the great building, a slight layer of dust coming off the walls as the wind invisibly ground down the yellow sandstone.

"Matthias!" a voice shouted from the courtyard. "Where are you?"

Matthias stepped behind one of the apple trees. Like many fifteen year olds his body hadn't quite finished growing but he had a lean and athletic poise. His dark hair swept around his face framing blue eyes and a wide full mouth.

He watched a young boy sit down on a low stone wall and breath a deep sigh, before shouting, "I give up!" to the skies. The youngster rested his head on his hands and his brown fringe dangled over his eyes. Matthias watched as he blew out from his mouth and for a moment the lock of hair hung in the air before dropping back.

Albert was thirteen years old but he looked younger. He was new to the abbey, small and sometimes got picked on, but usually the bigger boys left him alone. That was because he had made friends with Matthias and people tended to not get on the wrong side of Matthias.

Albert looked around again, his freckled cheeks gathered around his nose as he peered over at the tree. Matthias stepped out from behind the gnarled trunk.

"Prepare to be boarded!" yelled Matthias.

Albert leapt to his feet. "Stand fast men!" he bellowed. A bystander may have noticed a not very convincing French accent.

There was s shimmer of light from behind the tree and then the blur of colour.

"Surrender Captain Albert!"

"It's Alberrr...you don't pronounce the 'T.'"

Another flash of something. A coat? A head? Then suddenly Matthias was stood in front of Albert and the two boys presented their wooden swords.

"Whatever, surrender your vessel!"

"Never!"

Albert leapt toward Matthias dancing sideways until they were within each other's reach. The 'clonk' of sabres clashing was unmistakeable and the duel lasted sometime before Captain Alberrr, mortally wounded, plunged all of two feet to his death.

Albert rolled onto his knees and scowled at Matthias. "How do you do that?"

"What?" said Matthias, offering a hand.

"That thing, you know, when you move so quickly. I can hardly even see you."

Matthias regarded him with a quizzical look, his eyes narrowed and they gave his face a mischievous appearance. "I don't know what you mean."

The two started to make their way back to the Abbey. It was morning service soon and they had to be in the chapel. But Albert wasn't going to let the point go.

"Yes you do," he said, as they made their way through the giant stone archway and into the courtyard. "The way you move, it's not natural."

"I suppose I'm just very quick," said Matthias, slightly less assuredly. "I've always been quick. As long as I can remember."

Nudging him, Albert caught Matthias's eye and nodded to his left. It was Rebecca and Albert smiled awkwardly as she approached. Matthias's twin sister had eyes like pieces of sky breaking through dark clouds. Her light brown hair fell about her head and never really seemed to settle even when she was still. To Matthias though, all this was background to the look of worry she had on her face.

"What is it?"

"It happened again," she said.

"Where?"

Rebecca was visibly shaking and tears swelled in her eyes. "The store room. Please come quickly."

"Cover for me," said Matthias, before darting away with Rebecca. The two made their way around the back of the abbey to a large wooden shack at the side. As they approached Matthias could see smoke rising from underneath the door.

Rebecca started to break down and sob. "It was an accident. I don't know why it happens."

Matthias put his arm around her. "It's alright. Go and sit back in your room. I'll deal with this before Sister Helena finds out."

"I'm sorry."

"Don't worry. It's not your fault."

Rebecca hugged her brother and dashed off into the abbey. Matthias turned, breathed in and heaved open the door. Smoke surged outward briefly blinding him before subsiding to reveal the chaos within.

The storeroom was about twelve foot long and six foot wide filled with bags of grain, barrels and various boxes of food. The bags were singed black and glowing orange along the edges, the barrels were smouldering and in places there were small flames.

Rebecca, thought Matthias, *why does this happen?* He pounded at the flames licking the boxes as best he could with his coat. Slowly but surely he suffocated the fires but the smoke seemed to become more intense. Stepping back to the doorway he stopped to get his breath and cover his stinging eyes.

They were only just beginning to stop streaming when he was jolted by the slap of a hand on his shoulder and a shrill voice screamed in his ear. "Matthias!"

"Wh-what? Sister Helena?"

"What have you done?"

"It wasn't me. I – "

"You'll pay for this! Come with me," Sister Helena hissed, and Matthias felt a twitch run down his throat.

She grabbed his arm and started to half lead him, half drag him into the abbey. They made their way toward the refectory down a dim passageway lit by oil lamps. It seemed to Matthias as if the very flames themselves protested and shied away as Sister Helena stormed towards the office of Father James.

"What have I done, Sister?" But Matthias was not yet going to get an answer. The towering nun remained completely silent as she pulled him along the stone floors. From underneath the approaching door Matthias could see light. Father James was probably scribing again. The old jovial monk spent most of his time these days writing up sermons and holy works on parchment.

Sister Helena knocked three times but then proceeded to enter without waiting for a reply. She slammed the door behind her, nearly catching

Matthias in the act. The old monk sat hunched over his desk, the top of his quill wobbling across the paper in front of him. Then the feather fell still and was gently lowered.

"Come in," said Father James, with more than a little hint of mockery.

"I've just been to the storerooms," said Sister Helena, "There's been another fire!"

Father James sighed and the noise seemed to drag on for several seconds. He was still looking at his piece of parchment, although now his head was tilted at a more thoughtful angle than the normal craning he did over his beloved scriptures. Once, Matthias had been gifted a glimpse of the man's work and was astonished at the beauty and intricacy of colour the monk attended to each page. To him, it was holy work indeed.

"I'm guessing you have Matthias with you?" As he spoke Father James turned around on his stool wearily and his eyes caught Matthias's. He looked as if he wished that Matthias was not standing there before him, but unfortunately he was.

The monk was old but clearly still had his wits about him. White hair, save a bald patch on top, fell to his neck and his eyes were bright blue. His brown tunic was simple but dignified. Matthias had always thought of him as firm but fair and indeed had the sneaking suspicion that the old man actually held a soft spot for him. "Tell me boy."

"I don't know what Sister Helena is talking about."

"Liar!" shrieked the nun.

Father James sighed and leaned back in his chair. "Sister Helena," he began, "I'm sure you haven't bought Matthias here without some proof of his wrongdoings?"

"Indeed not," came the prompt reply, "I caught him red handed. It's still smoking in there. We've lost most of our grain and the fruit barrels."

"What were you doing by the store rooms?" asked the old monk.

"Looking for Albert."

"May I enquire as to why?" replied Father James, "If it is not too much trouble." He smiled and looked at Matthias, but all the while had one eyebrow raised. Whether it was mirth or his temper Matthias couldn't tell.

"We were playing a game," said Matthias, with ill-hid sarcasm.

Just for a second a smile seemed to crease at the edge of the monk's mouth. He continued, "And did you find Albert, Matthias?"

"No, but I found the fire and I put it out."

Sister Helena exploded. "How much of this nonsense must we hear?"

"Please, Sister," Father James said, "does Matthias not have a right to speak?"

Her body seemed to subside, but her eyes still looked like they might burst. Taking advantage of the silence Matthias continued. Slowly, and calculated as ever, he told them how he had gone to the stores to look for Albert as part of their elaborate war game; Albert was going to be defending the fort. He saw the smoke and decided to investigate himself rather than raising the alarm. He made sure they noted that he did so out of the interests of the rest of the children, in case the fire spread. He knew it was the right thing to do and he was only trying to be a 'good Samaritan.' This last part Matthias was secretly very smug about, as it had come from Father James's sermon on Wednesday.

Would Father James see through his tale? The answer became apparent as soon as the monk opened his mouth. He looked drily at Matthias and started clapping. "A fine yarn, Matthias. Worthy of one of the travelling bards I dare say."

A cold sweat suddenly crept over Matthias's skin. "But I know you and you know me," Father James continued. This was true; the two had often found themselves at loggerheads over the years discussing Matthias's discipline…or lack of it.

"I'm frankly rather insulted. This was not one of your better tales."

Sister Helena smiled; it wasn't pleasant to look at. Her eyes narrowed in triumph and she spoke swiftly, "What should I do with him Father? A thrashing?"

"Good Lord, no. Send him to the cellar without supper."

Sister Helena seemed mildly deflated, but grabbed Matthias and began to lead him out of the room nonetheless. They were halfway out of the door, Matthias scrambling in her grip as she pulled his collar, when Father James spoke. His face was already back in his parchments but the voice was loud and clear and this time sounded sharp as a blade.

"Matthias, was Rebecca anywhere near the stores?"

"No."

The monk appeared to ponder this answer for a moment. "Next time Matthias, try to be more creative. Despite being old I still remember sermons I gave less than a week ago." And with that, the door was shut and he was back outside in the torch lit corridor.

"Unbelievable," muttered Sister Helena under her breath. "Still, I'm sure sleeping in the cold with no food will help you see the error of your ways."

She dragged him down the corridor, past the classroom and towards the cellar. Opening the door she hurled him inside and slammed it shut. The last sound Matthias heard, was the turning of the old rusty key in the door and Sister Helena's snorting as she walked away into the darkness.

Chapter 2

Raindrops marched on the abbey roof. From the cellar below the classroom Matthias could hear water trickling above and every so often the growl of thunder. It was cold, so cold he could feel his feet starting to go numb. He cursed Sister Helena and vowed to exact some suitable revenge when he got out.

The abbey was his home but at times like this he almost wished it weren't. His mind drifted back to last year when three older children had left to take up positions with craftsmen. One of them, Thomas, Matthias had remembered especially well.

Tom had taken a liking to him for as long as either of them could remember. The big brother he never had, it was a sad day indeed to see Tom head off into the service of a nearby farmer with nothing but a smile and the clothes he stood in. As tiredness eventually overcame the cold and draughts, Matthias drifted off to sleep wondering what life lay ahead of him when he too would one day leave the abbey.

Would he end up ploughing fields or herding sheep? And what of Rebecca? A dairy maid? Or perhaps a servant in some manor house? The thought of being apart from her turned his stomach. Better that he make his own fortune and buy them a house together; then they would never be apart.

He had barely slept half an hour when a loud banging stirred him from his dreams. The classroom was located near the narthex, the large forum like entrance to the abbey, and the sound was being made by someone knocking on its great doors. As high as the ceilings themselves the doors required the strength of an elephant to shift and, from the noise he was hearing, Matthias was worried for a second that that was indeed the case. He heard Sister Helena approaching from above, muttering about the lateness of the hour, and imagined her face when a large elephant appeared from behind the doors. It made him smile and forget about the cold just for a moment.

After some murmured discussion Matthias heard the door open fully and then close again. Footsteps grew louder until the visitor and Sister Helena entered the classroom above. A man's voice spoke in a foreign accent.

"The Bishop was very insistent that I come under the circumstances but I do apologise for the lateness of the hour, Sister."

"Not at all, Signor. I'm afraid Father James has gone to the village though. I believe to read the last rites to a poor soul."

"So sad. Still, I am sure we can proceed without him. Is she here?"

"Yes, I'll just fetch her."

Sister Helena left the room and headed off to the dormitory. From above, footsteps circled impatiently. Matthias stood up on a chair so he could get a better view through the cracks in the floor. He could see most of the classroom and the robes of the man but couldn't make out his face. The stranger paced again around the classroom but stopped to inspect a pile of books. Finally the nun returned and from below Matthias could see his sister, bleary eyed, in tow.

"Ah, you must be?"

"Rebecca," she said, trying to disguise a yawn.

The man stepped slowly across the room towards her. Each footstep was accompanied by the sound of his boots hitting the floorboards and they creaked under his weight.

"Rebecca. Such a beautiful name. I believe we have been looking for each other."

"You have?" Sister Helena seemed affronted she was not privy to the news.

"Why indeed. I was acquainted with this young lady's mother, a long time ago. You see Rebecca, she too had a gift. A gift that was sometimes impossible to control. Do you know what I am talking about?"

The man kneeled down in front of Rebecca and Matthias could make out Sister Helena turning her head. "Gift? What is the meaning of this?"

"Hush now Sister, I was talking to Rebecca. Tell me, can you command fire?"

Matthias managed to gently prise up a loose floorboard so that his brow and eyes poked into the room. Rebecca had started to wobble on her feet and even though she hadn't noticed her brother her eyes told Matthias she was frightened. He clenched his fists in anger. *Damn Sister Helena for locking me in here!*

"Perhaps," continued the man, "you need some coercion, no?" His hand dropped to his side and he slowly pulled out a dagger. Rebecca stepped back, her legs hitting a chair and moving it nosily.

"Now look here," began Sister Helen but before she could finish the man had stood up and was holding the blade at her throat.

"Be still Sister. Now, Rebecca, tell me. Can you command fire?"

She shook her head and took another step back, her hand reaching for the chair behind her. Suddenly there was a whooshing sound like a wind and then an orange glow grew through the cracks all around Matthias. The chair had caught fire!

From below he saw Rebecca look at her hand aghast and the man grinned. "So, you *are* Margaret's daughter."

"Rebecca! Run!" said Sister Helena. She managed to squirm out of the man's hold and push Rebecca towards the door but then she froze before finally falling to the floor. The man had killed her!

Matthias nearly fell off the stool. Should he move? Should he let the man know he was here? There was nothing he could do - he was locked in the cellar below! Rebecca was stood with her back to the door, her poor eyes now wide and helpless.

"Come here child." One hand was reaching out to her, the blood red dripping dagger still held in the other. Matthias moved across a floor board so that he might see further along the room. Behind Rebecca the doorway erupted in flames.

As she stood there, framed by fires, the stranger got closer and closer. Finally he reached out and pulled her toward him.

"Hush now," he said, and held her close. Matthias heard a slight noise, much like a whimper of an animal before the man gently rolled his sister onto the floor at his side. Flames started to climb the walls, the crackling sound now accompanied by leaping sparks. Rebecca lay still.

Matthias felt his heart muscling its way out of his chest. His mouth was open to scream but there was no sound coming out. *Rebecca!* Footsteps echoed away and the classroom door slammed shut. The only sound he could hear was the snapping of the fires.

He dropped to the floor on his knees and was sick. Tears and spittle dripped to the stones and he let out a guttural wail. He breathed in quickly in short sharp breaths before curling up on the floor in a ball. For minutes he lay there. Then, he started to hear the screams.

It was one or two at first. Matthias presumed they had heard the fire but he was not concerned. He would gladly lay here and burn. *Rebecca!*

But then more screams. Running, chairs and tables crashing. He looked up, trying to place the sounds. Through the floorboards he could see the classroom was ablaze now and smoke was starting to fill the cellar. Footsteps approached the door above and it burst open. A shadow came crashing through the flames. Then more footsteps; slower, heavier, more deliberate.

Matthias crept back up onto the chair. As he raised himself on his tiptoes he could make out the stranger at the door with a sword in his hand. Albert was stood in front of him, motionless. The flames had started to drift up to the ceiling and the light caught the steel of the blade.

The man lunged forward and grabbed Albert; running him through. After stumbling for a few steps the boy finally tumbled to the floor like a wounded animal and lay still.

Matthias watched the man walk around the classroom. He was looking for something, but Matthias couldn't tell what. He picked up some books and flicked through some papers and opened a draw at the front that contained the class register. Fourteen names in all, perhaps now most of them were dead?

"Matthias." The work echoed down through the floorboards and seemed to bounce around the cellar. He started to shake and immediately look for a way out. There was none.

"Matthias!"

The man was shouting indiscriminately now, perhaps aware the boy was hiding and trying to lure him out. He went back out into the corridor and shouted again before Matthias heard his footsteps running off.

Above him flames crackled and timbers started to groan. The whole of the classroom was on fire and, by the sounds of it, the rest of the abbey too. He looked around at the cellar once more. The only door was thick and locked. Some tables, chairs and wood were stacked high; once they started to burn he was finished. His only chance was to somehow get through the floor to the classroom above; but how?

Then he noticed the fireplace. Old and dirty at the back it was never used but the chimney connected to the one above and beyond that to the roof of the castle. He made for it and instantly started to shimmy up the inside, legs and feet gripping the dusty and dirty walls where they could.

As he reached the ground floor he saw light coming through from the room above. His mind raced as he decided the best course of action. Out through the fireplace into the burning classroom were the man had been searching and perhaps still was, or to the roof?

In the end he took his chances and eased himself through the fireplace. As he landed on the floor it groaned loudly and he noticed that the boards were beginning to take to the flame. The chairs and desks were upturned and either ablaze already or starting to smoulder.

Rebecca was lying in the middle of the room and Matthias rushed to her. Picking up her head in his hands he looked into her eyes which, until moments ago, had been the brightest things in the world. He sobbed and clutched her head to his stomach.

"Rebecca."

He laid her head carefully on the floor, stroked some of her hair back out of her face and kissed her on the cheek. A loud crack made him look towards the door frame which was sagging precariously and burning with a hot orange flame. He stood up and made for the window.

As he neared it he picked up a chair leg, looked around once more in case the man was still nearby, and then smashed the glass. It shattered into pieces but large shards remained attached to the timbers.

Coughing and covering his eyes Matthias took one last look at his sister and then jumped up and through the window frame slicing his arms and hands as he did.

As he ran from the abbey for the cover of some nearby trees he looked back and was shocked to see most of the building on the west side now ablaze. Outside the doors were bodies and he could just make out a lone rider galloping away down the path towards the main road.

He stared at the unholy blaze before him. The blackened skeleton of the abbey could be seen through the bright yellow flames that licked the sky. A timber on the east wing roared and gave way, swiftly followed by the rest of the chapel roof. At one point he looked around the grounds for survivors, but found none. Everybody must have been inside. In their beds, or perhaps the stranger had found them.

How long he stood there, watching the fire slowly devouring the once great building, he didn't know. Finally, only the glowing orange remnants of the timbers smouldered and he sat down on the grass. The sun was rising but it could barely be seen through the thick smoke that hung in the air. Eventually ash started to drift down from the sky like snow. He was alone. There was nobody else here and for the first time in his life he felt frightened.

Rebecca was gone. Albert was gone. The other children, the nuns even Father James. Holding himself tight he thought only of his sister. He recalled her face as the man advanced on her. Why hadn't he cried out? He should have done something, anything. But it was no use, he told himself, he would have been killed too.

Standing up he decided his only option was to head to the local village. The smoke could be seen for miles around in the dawn's light he guessed so no doubt some villagers would be on their way to investigate. Indeed he had only been walking for a few minutes down the hard dirt track when he came upon one such individual…or so he thought.

The man was tall and wide as a barrel. The wind blew his long black hair out underneath a tall hat. A great coat was flapping behind him and as he drew closer Matthias saw he had a patch over his left eye. Matthias noted his dusty clothes and presumed him to be a traveller.

"Quickly boy, I am looking for the abbey?"

"It's gone."

"Gone? Gone where?"

"It burnt down."

"What? When?" his voice was heavily accented, Matthias couldn't tell from where but it was similar to the stranger's at the abbey. The one eyed stranger looked up and noticed the great columns of black smoke for the first time. "Good God," he said, slowly under his breath.

For some moments the man regarded the scene breathing deeply and then finally looking back at Matthias. "I was looking for someone."

"There's nobody left. Father James, Sister Helena...they're all gone."

"I was looking for a boy named Matthias. Do you know him?"

Matthias froze but his mind raced rapidly. He'd never seen the man before, he was certain of it and the accent meant he was not from the village. Then he noticed a dagger at the stranger's belt. Silver with a black stone set in the hilt his eyes looked at it then the man's grizzled face, but it was too late, he'd guessed.

"You're Matthias aren't you?"

Matthias said nothing.

"Yes you are. Of course you are. Don't be afraid. My name is Alonso. It is a Spanish name. I am a mystic like my father before me and I'm here to help you"

Chapter 3

Something in the stranger's voice told Matthias to trust him. He started to lead the way back to the village, turning once to see if Matthias followed. As the man looked back along the track the last remnants of Matthias's energy shifted his steps and he started to walk.

His feet dragged, his shoulders hung but he managed to keep his eyes on the man Alonso. The village was only a mile away and normally reachable in fifteen minutes but it took them over thirty to get to the outskirts.

Matthias, who had been silent all the way, had no real recollection of the journey. Walking into the village inn, which was busy serving up breakfast to hungry travellers, he barely noticed a hunched figure sat in the corner turn to look as he took a seat next to the fire. As the Spaniard ordered some ale and meats the figure raised a hooded head.

"Matthias?"

He barely registered the noise; staring into the flames as they licked greedily at fresh logs, his thoughts were only of Rebecca.

"Matthias?" The figure had stood up now and was lurching toward him, with one arm outstretched.

Finally, registering his name, he looked up and gasped. *The devil from the abbey?* He recoiled as the figure stepped forward to the table, reaching out. In a blur of movement Alonso had upended the table, a sword held to the man's throat. The inn fell into silence and Alonso pulled back the cowl covering the man's face. It was Father James.

"Alonso, it's me!" said the monk. The mystic stepped back, sheathing his sword.

"My apologies father," said the Spaniard.

"What are you doing here? What is going on?"

Father James sat down next to Matthias. For the first time he noticed his own skin was black and his clothes torn and bloodied.

"What has happened?" said the monk.

Slowly, and not leaving out any detail, Matthias told him. At the part of the story were Rebecca had been killed he broke down and Father James had to hold him, tears dripping from his own cheeks.

The two of them sat alone for several minutes and it was a long time before Alonso finally spoke.

"Tonight you will stay here," he said, "I will go to fetch assistance. For now, to your rooms and pray rest."

As the giant man stood up he ducked his head beneath an oak beam attracting the looks of several surprised farmers. He walked to the bar, spoke briefly with the landlord and then walked over to Matthias and Father James.

"Who are you?" said Matthias, "and how do you know Father James?"

"I serve the duke," said Alonso.

The monk placed an arm around Matthias and held him; it didn't occur to him to ask who the duke was. The two went up to a room above the stables, but of course no rest came for either of them. Matthias lay on one of the beds whilst Father James sat at the window waiting for daylight.

The sheets were soft and thick and he pulled them tight around him. He closed his eyes but could still see the burning abbey and then, through the fires, Rebecca's eyes staring back from an inferno.

For many hours Matthias tried to sleep. Time after time he felt his eyelids close but each time he woke with a start. On one such occasion he felt the cold hand of Father James on his forehead.

"Who was that man, Father?"

"Alonso is an acquaintance of mine from many years ago. We…lost touch it would be fair to say."

"He said he was looking for me. Who is he?"

"We'll talk later. For now, try to sleep."

The hand stroked his forehead, moving a lock of hair across tenderly. Tiredness finally overcame him and he must have fallen asleep as when he next opened his eyes it was dark. The evening had come and with it news, in the form of a maid telling them they were wanted downstairs. They made their way back to the bar room where Alonso was waiting; he gestured to some seats at a table with food. They sat down but neither ate and Alonso informed them that a Mr Hardy was just outside saddling his horse.

The door opened and cold evening air flooded in. The gentleman entered wrapped in a travelling cloak and he was followed by two other men; both armed with swords and dressed in plain black livery.

He sat himself down opposite them whilst the two men remained at the door. He was a handsome man; in his forties perhaps. A big black moustache drew the onlooker's attention to the centre of a strong face. His smile was warm and genuine and he immediately made Matthias feel at ease.

Father James looked up weakly with tears in his eyes. He looked older. He took Matthias's hand and they found some comfort in the warmth of each other's touch.

The gentleman smiled, but sadly. "James, it's been a long time."

"Mr Hardy."

"You must be Matthias?" The man regarded him with a fascinated stare before patting his hand softly. "I am Mr Hardy, Master of the Sandstone Castle."

"You know each other?" said Matthias.

"I've known James for many years now. I was also a friend of your father's."

"Mr Hardy, this is not the time."

Father James had raised himself in his seat, his eyes never leaving the gentleman sat across from him.

"If we are to go to Sandstone Castle, does the boy not need to know who he is?"

After some thought Father James nodded. Most of the other diners had left now and the room was all but empty. The three men sat around the table; the Spaniard sitting at the bar and the innkeeper were the only others present.

"Alonso," said Mr Hardy, "let us have some privacy."

The Spaniard said something to the landlord and gave him a coin. The man promptly cast a quick look over his establishment before disappearing into the back rooms. Mr Hardy nodded to the guards at the door and they too left, but Matthias only heard a couple of steps after the door had closed.

Father James looked at Mr Hardy who nodded his approval before clearing his throat and speaking. "Matthias, you are not the son of a farmer. You're real name is Matthias Cortés."

For a moment Matthias couldn't make sense of the words; it almost seemed like they had gone in and out of his head and he had only caught the gist. He stared back at his uncle.

"Your father was Michael Cortés, son of Hernan Cortés and husband of Margaret. He was my brother."

Matthias leant back in his seat, the two front legs lifting off the floor. "You're my uncle?"

"Please. Can you give us a moment alone?" Father James said to Mr Hardy.

"Of course," said Mr Hardy. He led Alonso outside, gently closing the door behind him.

"My dear boy", said Father James, holding Matthias's hand. "I am afraid none of this is how it was supposed to be." He made an empty gesture at the heavens. "Your father never wanted you to end up involved in all of this.

"He wanted to protect you. He made me swear to keep you safe and never let you to be touched by this dark world. He wanted you to live a long, happy, but largely ignorant life. And for all these years I kept my promise."

"What happened to him?"

The old monk looked down as he spoke. "Not long after you were born our father, your grandfather, arrived at the abbey. He brought you and your sister with him and he told me that your mother, Margaret, had been murdered. He asked me to look after you both whilst Michael went to avenge her death. He never returned. Shortly afterwards a messenger brought this ring to the duke."

Father James extended out his hand to show the sovereign ring on his smallest finger he had worn ever since Matthias had known him. It was intricate gold, with a solitary coin on top.

"This was your father's ring. It is our family crest and the seal of Cortés."

Matthias sat in contemplation for some time but after a while started to feel restless. He stood up and walked over to the smouldering fireplace. Absent-mindedly he played with the poker stirring up the coals. Sparks briefly crackled but were quickly smothered by the ash.

"What is to happen to me?"

"I believe Mr Hardy would like us to return with him to the Sandstone Castle, a fortress where the duke trains his young soldiers, some of them children even younger than you."

"An army?"

"A force, called 'The Guard,' who serve the duke; your father was a captain."

"Who are they fighting?"

"The Legion. The Guard and the Legion are two groups of vast and powerful families at war with each other. Make no mistake though; the Guard strive to rid our lands of a great evil in the Legion. What you saw yesterday is an example of their most dastardly work."

Matthias's thoughts immediately returned to Rebecca. He breathed deeply and steadied himself on the inglenook. *Why? Why had they been dragged into this? Why Rebecca?* He asked his uncle.

"I cannot say. Perhaps Mr Hardy can enlighten us. Maybe they found out who you were? Your sister's gift…It had attracted a certain amount of unwanted attention."

At the mention of the word 'gift' Matthias turned to look at the monk.

"The castle is a school for special children. Gifted children. You are such a child and so was your sister. Her gift was the ability to conjure fire from thin air. Your gift is your speed. You are probably the quickest child I have ever seen; don't think nobody noticed."

There was the faintest of taps at the door and Mr Hardy put his head inside. Father James beckoned him over and he came and sat at the table; Alonso followed but remained standing.

"What happens now?" said Father James

"He knows?"

"Yes."

"For now, I would suggest we head back to the castle where it is safe. We can talk more there about our next steps."

The monk turned away, the firelight showing the shadows of tear stains on his smock. "When must we go?"

Alonso spoke. "Immediately. You may still be in danger."

After some deep breaths they stood up, pulled on their cloaks and walked to the door. The two powerful looking men outside had eyes like hunters; Matthias noticed their gazes sweeping the courtyard and landscape as they all made their way to the awaiting carriage. The men produced rifles from somewhere and leapt on top. Mr Hardy stepped inside and Alonso shut the door on Matthias and Father James before bidding them farewell.

"Alonso," said Mr Hardy, "The matter we discussed earlier. Please make sure my instructions are carried out to the letter. The trail grows colder as we speak. If you find him…we need him alive."

"Yes. I understand," said Alonso. His eyes dropped and Matthias heard a slight sigh.

"Of course," said Mr Hardy, "I leave the definition of 'alive' entirely up to you." The gentleman urged the driver to depart.

As they rode away Alonso faded into the giant shadow of an overhanging tree, but two small twinkles of light could be seen for a split second and Matthias saw them both. One was the moonlight reflecting on the Spaniard's blade as he pulled it from his belt. The other was the faintest flash of his white teeth.

They rode on in silence for several hours. Nobody had anything to say but Matthias couldn't possibly sleep. Each time he felt his head nod through sheer exhaustion the face of Rebecca would leap out from the darkness at him. What was this madness? How could such evil exist? He hoped Mr Hardy could answer some of his questions.

The gentleman looked sullen and ill at ease as he sat in the coach, the breeze buffeting one side of his face. His curly hair was swept back behind a thick hat atop which sat a silver buckle. In one hand he held a black wooden cane which he idly toyed with, staring out of the carriage window into the passing countryside.

"Mr Hardy?" whispered Matthias. The man looked at him with a start. Maybe he had been falling asleep. It had been a long night for them all and it was nearly morning.

"What is it?" he asked. "Is everything alright?"

"Yes. I just wanted to speak with you."

Mr Hardy sat up, and looked attentive. "I will try to answer your questions as honestly as I can."

"Tell me about them. About the Legion."

"To understand the Legion you must first understand the duke." Mr Hardy paused to take a look at the monk sat next to Matthias. Satisfied Father James was asleep, he continued.

"His Grace was a noble adventurer from Spain. One of the boldest of all time! He and his men made a great journey across the ocean and discovered a far off land. And with it a secret. A fantastic secret."

"What was the secret?" asked Matthias.

"Not many can say for sure. But it changed them and it changed their children."

"Changed them?"

"Yes." Mr Hardy leaned closer. "Matthias, did your uncle explain you were special? Like all the children in our castle?"

Matthias's head was starting to turn over again. He felt he was grasping something but he wasn't quite sure what it was.

"Yes…I am quick."

Mr Hardy stifled a chuckle. "But how quick? Has it never occurred to you as you were growing up that you were so much quicker than the other children? Did you not play games and find them easier? Beat boys twice your size and age at sports?"

"Yes. But it came naturally to me."

"It is in your blood. You too, like the other children in the castle, are a descendant of the true scions. What happened to them, happened to their sons, grandsons and everyone who came afterwards." With this last comment he pointed a gloved finger at Matthias.

"Grandson. I am the duke's grandson."

"Yes. Your father was Michael Cortés, the duke's son." Mr Hardy's eyes narrowed for a second as he gauged the reaction from Matthias.

Matthias sat back in his seat. He wasn't sure he was fit to continue the conversation. He had grown up without any family except Rebecca and now, within the space of a day, he had learned he had a father, a murdered mother, an uncle who had watched over him in secret all his life and now a duke for a grandfather.

A thought occurred to him. He tilted his head toward Father James. "So why was he –"

"In the abbey?" said the monk, before Matthias could finish his sentence.

Mr Hardy chuckled. "So James, you weren't asleep after all then? I hope you don't mind me filling Matthias in on some of your family history"

"Not at all. As long as it is a balanced view I have no complaint."

The two men regarded each other as the coach continued to trundle. It was raining outside now and the noise on the roof made it hard to be heard. Father James had to increase the volume of his voice and it made Matthias start.

"I am afraid my father and I don't get along. I serve the Lord, whereas he believes I should serve him. I am a man of peace, not violence."

"Neither is your father, sir," said Mr Hardy. "He uses the sword only to defend his family and those under his protection."

"My father trains children to kill. I don't care whether it is for their own protection or not. Using an innocent child as a weapon of war is a sin in the eyes of our Lord."

Matthias looked at the monk and spoke softly. "Maybe if they had been trained in the abbey they would have been able to defend themselves?"

Father James turned swiftly on Matthias, his eyes wide and red. "I had those children taken away for their protection before my father could get his hands on them. They were orphans. They needed comfort and guidance; not to be set loose as killers!"

Mr Hardy cleared his throat. "That isn't a word we like to use, James."

"I thought you said the children were training to be soldiers?" Matthias asked.

Mr Hardy smiled, "Matthias, you must understand ours is a secret war. We do not fight on battlefields. We fight in the shadows. In the council chambers and amongst the politicians. The castle is merely a training ground to prepare our agents for their work."

"So who are the Legion?"

The gentleman looked at Father James and raised an eyebrow as if to ask for permission to continue. The monk exhaled and sat back in his chair.

"You see," said Mr Hardy, "your grandfather was with five other Spanish noblemen when they stumbled upon the secret. But they couldn't agree on what to do with it.

"The six men came to blows and fought as they argued over whether to share their mysterious treasure with the world or to present it to the King of Spain. The duke and his two friends said it was too dangerous, whereas the others believed that Spain could conquer the world by means of the secret. And so, after a bitter feud, the duke and his friends hid forever what they had found, telling no-one. Vasco and his allies have been after it ever since."

"Vasco?"

"Vasco Nunez. Six great families took up arms against each other. On one side the houses of Pizarro, de Ojeda and Legazpi aligned to the duke. And the other side the houses of Balboa, de Soto and Nunez." As he said the last name he spat on the floor with disgust. "We believe the attack on the abbey was carried out by a member of the Nunez family. A man by the name of Balthazar."

"How do you know it was this man?" Matthias asked, rage already inside him now he had a name to connect it to.

"Alonso asked around the village. It would seem he ate at the very inn we were in the day before. From his description and some questioning of the locals we are quite sure."

"Where is he?"

"We do not know, but Alonso is on his trail. Unfortunately for Nunez our mystic has taken very badly to what happened at the abbey and swore an oath to bring the man to justice. If I were Balthazar Nunez I would pray death finds me first. Alonso is very skilled with a blade. He can make someone suffer for quite a considerable length of time."

Matthias thought of the wicked smile he saw on the Spaniard's face as they had left the village. His head leaned against the carriage wall and his mind span with thoughts of the duke, his family, the war and finally his sister who died without knowing any of this. He must have drifted into some form of sleep because when he was woken by Father James it was daylight but they were under a great shadow.

He shifted over to the nearest side of the carriage and stuck out his head. Immediately he was hit by the blinding light of the sun. Squinting, he held his hand over his eyes as they grew accustomed to the daylight. The wind blew across his face clearing his mind and sight in one hit, but nothing could prepare him for what he saw.

They were on a dirt track at the foot of a great hill around which sprawled a patchwork of farm fields. Every so often there was a solitary farmhouse, smoke trickling upwards from thatched roofs. A hamlet, Matthias speculated, where the farmers paid rent to the duke for use of the fertile land. Over to his right was a thick forest that had so many trees you could barely see into it much beyond the large old oaks that stood at the edge like guardians, and on the left a large river busily made its way past. But all this was overshadowed by a great castle, the like of which Matthias had never imagined in all his dreams.

Imposing dark towers of stone seemed to grow out of the very ground itself. All the way up the stained glass windows were lit from behind by the setting sun and seemed to project the multitude of coloured light outward into the valley like a rainbow. It must have been ten, no twenty, times the size of the abbey and as they neared it the light from the windows bowed down to the enormous shadow of the castle itself. Matthias was still hanging out of the carriage door and staring in awe as they passed twenty foot black iron doors that sat in the middle of the front wall. The carriage continued around the side of the castle through a smaller entrance. Inside, a large stables, warehouses and servants quarters all appeared in what amounted to a small village on top of the hill.

They came to a halt and Mr Hardy gestured for him to exit. Opening the door Matthias was met by a boy who set a wooden box under the door to allow him to descend with ease. The boy, who was dressed in a smart black tabard, stood to one side.

"Is this where the duke lives?"

The boy stood by the carriage snorted with laughter and Matthias felt the skin on his face go red.

"Come now, Harry. We'll have less of that. Matthias, allow me to introduce your new roommate,

Harry. He is a new arrival like you, even though he pretends not to be."

The young boy's hands instantly whipped to his side to attention like a soldier and the smirk vanished from his face. Matthias got a chance to take look at him. He had strong features and was bigger, but he also had a boyish nature on the face underneath golden brown hair which made Matthias think he was younger than he looked. His eyes gazed into the distance as he awaited a command.

"Indeed," continued Mr Hardy, "Harry was so much of an expert when he arrived that he found his way to the latrines when he was looking for the storerooms. A mistake I am sure he will not be repeating, certainly not now he finds the time to mock others. Will you, Harry?"

"No, Mr Hardy," was the sorrowful reply. The shoulders shrugged a little and it was clear he too was now every bit as embarrassed as Matthias had been.

"Harry will take you to your quarters and then I want you both in the mustering hall within the hour. Is that clear?"

"Yes, Mr Hardy," said Harry.

The gentleman disappeared and left the two boys alone. Harry gave Matthias a wink and said, "Come on then!" before darting toward a door and into the castle. Matthias followed.

The walls were bare stone, plastered in places, but for the main old and crumbling. Here and there oil lanterns lit the way and as he walked past door after door, corridor after corridor, Matthias was already feeling lost.

Finally they turned a corner and walked into a large hall. Several rows of tables and benches, at which sat children of various ages reading, eating or just playing games. At one table a couple of older boys were playing chess, at a second three girls were spinning wool whilst another read from her book and at one table Matthias thought he caught a glimpse of an older boy hiding something quickly in his coat. Fierce green eyes caught Matthias's and it was clear he had noted an intrusion into his privacy.

They made their way to a corridor that led off the back before Harry opened the door to a small chamber.

"Our room," said Harry. "Your things are in the trunk. We just passed through the mustering hall out there. I've got to finish my studying." He scurried out of the door in a hurry.

Through the solitary window in the room enough light was let in to allow Matthias to inspect his surroundings in detail and his eyes fell immediately to the trunk. He opened it, expecting to see servant's tabards or leather work clothes but was surprised to find the same black velvet outfit he had seen Harry in. Come to think of it, most of the other children back in the hall too. Was he not to work the land? Or take care of the animals? Work in the forest perhaps or look after game?

But then Father James's words in the carriage came back to him. *Training children as soldiers?* Was that what the monk had said? Matthias must have misheard. He was tired and had been half asleep during the journey.

He took off his clothes and placed them carefully in the trunk; all the while at the back of his mind he retained the thought of needing them in case things didn't work out. The abbey was all he had ever known and somehow putting his shirt and pants at the bottom of the trunk filled him with sorrow. He knew he could never go back. He finished putting on the black tabard and noted the coat of arms in silver thread sewn into the chest of the clothing. Three swords over a fountain, surrounded by a shield.

Chapter 4

Dressed in his new black livery Matthias entered the mustering hall and took in the scene he hadn't had a chance to fully examine when he was last hurried through. The duke's shield hung on each corner of the large stone room, which had no windows but was lit by a giant chandelier hung from the ceiling. Four long tables dominated; each with benches running along its sides and children sat in groups talking or playing games. For a moment several pairs of eyes flicked upwards to look at him, but then each returned to whatever was occupying them before. Nobody, it seemed, wanted to even acknowledge he had entered the room.

Closest to him, reading on his own, was Harry. Further along the table sat a young girl also reading and at the other end a group of boys who looked like they were examining some tools in a box. A few younger children entered and left; all wearing the same black tabards and all ignoring Matthias. Some exchanged pleasantries with each other, but that was it. Gone was the 'chitter-chatter' of the abbey. No songs or laughter here. All the children seemed eerily quiet, almost as if Sister Helena was watching them. It was uncomfortable and Matthias decided to try and strike up a conversation when he sat down next to Harry.

"How long have you been here?" he asked.

Harry stared at the small book before him and, without looking away from the pages replied, "About a month."

"What kind of work do you do?" continued Matthias, relieved he had even got a response.

"Work?" he scoffed. "We don't work here. We learn."

"I see," responded Matthias, "so you're training. Is that what you're reading?"

"It's what I'm *trying* to read."

"I'd leave Harry alone if I were you", said another, softer, voice.

Matthias looked up to see the girl opposite had put down her book and was addressing him.

"He's got to learn the name of every organ in the human body by supper and he's struggling."

Harry scoffed again, but the girl continued. "Harry can be a real bore sometimes. My name is Sophie."

"Matthias." As he spoke he looked at her face. It was soft and slender; her eyes, although dark, shone like morning dew. Her straight black hair fell over her livery and blended in with the soft velvet. She stood up and walked over to him to shake hands; she was a little shorter than Matthias but seemed around the same age.

"Welcome. Have you just got here?"

"Yes," he replied, "I lost my home. Alonso and Mr Hardy brought me here."

"So you were *asked* to come here? You were not sent by your parents or guardians?"

"No," said Matthias, "I came from an abbey. We were all orphans. Why? How did you get here?"

The girl tilted her head, "My family organised it. For them, it is the greatest honour to have me accepted. This place is a school. We learn so we can enter the duke's service."

"Learn what though? Reading? Why do we need to read if we are to be soldiers?"

"Soldiers? Whatever gave you that idea?" asked Sophie, with curiosity.

"I thought that's what this place was. Aren't we to be trained as an army?"

Again Sophie laughed and her eyes lit up her face.

"Why would my family pay for me to be trained as a soldier?"

Her chuckles had attracted the attention of the group of boys across the room. They began to walk around the table to stand the other side of Matthias. One of them, the tallest asked, "What's the joke, Sophie?"

She looked up and, for a split second, her laughter stopped and was replaced by a scowl. Only Matthias noticed when the smile instantly returned but somehow it seemed forced.

"He thinks he's being trained to be a soldier."

The boy smirked, which was unpleasant to say the least. He was older and bigger than Matthias and looked mean. His face was pale but strong and he had short dark cropped hair. When he spoke, it was with disdain and disgust.

"Then he must be some sort of fool." His accent was aristocratic and his tone resonated menace. As Matthias turned to look at him he noticed a dagger sitting in the boy's belt, just like Alonso had worn, the handle glimmering savagely in the candlelight.

"What did you say?" Matthias asked, lifting his eyes.

The boy smiled, and then leaned down so his face was inches away. Nose to nose the boy hissed heavily and slowly, "I said you were a fool."

Matthias stared back at him, his eyes glaring but calm. Then suddenly, from nowhere, came a voice.

"I wouldn't do that if I were you, Gerard." Both boys turned to look. Standing in the doorway of the mustering hall was the owner of the thickly accented voice that had spoken. Alonso, stood next to Mr Hardy, who was looking faintly amused. Alonso himself, however, seemed most sombre.

"He's quick. Quicker than you I dare say. I wouldn't agitate him. He's confused and he is probably slightly frightened; which makes him dangerous. I would say he could take your blade and strike you down before you could blink."

Gerard stepped back from Matthias, looking suddenly alarmed. But just as quickly he regained his composure and gave a snort of distaste.

"Oh, you can scoff away, but I assure you he speaks the truth." Mr Hardy's eloquent voice continued. "In fact, Matthias, I'm sure we'd all love to see just how quick you are."

Blood rushed through Matthias and he felt a pulse of fear and excitement surge though his arms and legs. His eyes returned to Gerard's. There was the merest hint of uncertainty in them now and Matthias stared intently whilst calculating the distance of the knife from the corner of his own eye.

"He doesn't look quick to me," said Gerard.

Matthias felt like he was going to burst. He wanted to grab the knife and teach the boy a lesson. Something inside of him told him to wait. This was not right, not with all these people watching. An inner battle raged within as he resisted the temptation not to attack.

But then, and it all happened so quickly, he found himself holding the knife to the boy's throat. Had he just grabbed it whilst the lad struggled to step back? Had he pulled it up with one swift motion? Was it now held tightly against Gerard's skin, a small droplet of blood making its way along the edge of the blade to the hilt?

Gerard's mouth was open and his face was white. He had barely enough time to take a breath and was clearly stunned by Matthias's speed and reflexes. He looked Matthias dead in the eye before his own eyes started to frantically search the room, looking for help or a way out of the situation. There was none.

All the children sat in silence, watching. Mr Hardy's wry smirk had gone, only leaving traces of his bemusement. All the while next to him Alonso looked on, the single eye taking in every minute detail of the scene.

"Who's the fool now?" Matthias asked, through gritted teeth.

Gerard looked back with horror. "Who are you?"

"No one to be trifled with," said Matthias, in a soft whisper. "You had best remember that."

"That's enough now, Matthias," said Alonso. The words were spoken softly, but the voice commanded respect. He slipped the knife away from Gerard's neck, wiped the blood on his sleeve and then offered it back, handle first.

"Now," continued Alonso, "I think you had best come with Mr Hardy and me so we can have a talk and explain a little bit about where you are."

Matthias turned and walked toward the door. All the children sat, open mouthed, watching him as he left; some shuffled awkwardly in their seats as he walked past. Harry put down his book with a smirk whilst Sophie regarded him with fascination. She smiled her dazzling smile and caught his eye as he left to follow Alonso and Hardy.

Chapter 5

The lamp in the corner of the room lit Mr Hardy and Alonso from behind, casting their faces in shadow, and Matthias struggled to see their expressions as first Mr Hardy spoke.

"You see, Matthias," he began, "you *can* be trained here. As a member of the Guard you will take up arms in our war which is now, sadly, yours too."

The gentleman leaned forward, his elegant cuffs brushing the desk. "Everyone here in this castle serves the duke and his cause. Some have served for many years, and plenty have given their lives. We ask you to join us."

"Why me?" he asked.

"You are special," Alonso said. "In all my journeys around the empires I search for special children; gifted children. You are such a child. Your particular gift is your speed. You are probably the quickest child I have ever seen.

"Others have different gifts. Mr Hardy, for example, can pick off a butterfly's wing with a rifle from over three hundred yards. His sight is extraordinary, and matched with his aim gives him his 'gift'. Some of the children here can scale fortress walls, throw a man twice their size to the other side of the room, or creep up and slit your throat whilst you were standing in broad daylight.

"This is a school to focus those skills, learn others and from others. You will become a devastating weapon to help fight against a great evil that has plagued this land for too long. You *will* learn to kill."

Matthias looked at the lamp in the corner of the room. Watched it flicker from yellow to orange and then back.

Mr Hardy spoke again. "I realise this is all a lot to take in. Normally we take children who have been brought up by parents aligned to the duke. They send their sons and daughters to us to train and stand beside them. Your case is unusual, but not unheard of."

"They all have chosen to come here?" said Matthias.

"Yes," said Mr Hardy. "Whereas you were…found."

"You must understand it was no coincidence I was at the abbey," said Alonso. "As a mystic, my visions take me many places in search of individuals such as you. I am often disappointed, but not always. Shortly before you I *found* one other child this way. His name is Harry."

"I've met him."

"Harry is finding it all a little difficult too," said Mr Hardy. "Alonso discovered him in a village in the north. He had become quite a local legend with his hunting skills.

"Harry was able to creep up on game until he was literally on top of it," said the mystic. "It is possible to approach a man without him being aware, but to get that close to deer or boar was unheard of."

He toyed with the knife on his belt absent-mindedly. Just for a brief second the light from the lamp caught the silver and it flashed. The large oak chair creaked as he leaned on it and spoke softly. "Harry could have crept into this room behind you right now and you wouldn't have heard him."

Matthias turned around but there was only the solid wooden door with the iron key inside. The trembling light cast the silhouettes of Mr Hardy and Alonso onto the wood and he swallowed hard before turning to face them.

Mr Hardy sighed. "Local rumour, gossip in the village; people with your gifts do not stay anonymous for long. Your sister possessed a *very* special gift. Without our help she couldn't learn to control it and so..."

Their help? Could they have helped? If Rebecca had been able to control her gift, disguise it, maybe the Legion wouldn't have found her. Perhaps she would still be alive. If they had taught her, turned her power into something she could have used to defend herself. A look flashed across his face as he thought how this could so easily of been the case. But his uncle had kept him and his sister away from this world. Away from a world of war and murder. But it had hunted them down.

And now he wanted to turn and hunt the hunter. Find this man Nunez and kill him. But where and how he had no idea. Was this castle the place to start? Or should he just leave and go find him on his own. He was certain he would recognise the man if he saw him again. The eyes; pale blue, bright but somehow lifeless.

Matthias's own eyes glistened before he turned away to look at the floor. "What if I don't want to fight in your war?"

Mr Hardy smiled in a charming but ever so slightly sinister way. "My boy, a most poignant question. Why should you indeed take up arms or even lay down your life for this cause?"

"Why indeed," said Alonso. He stood up and made his way to the fire burning on the other side of the room. He placed one great hand on the mantelpiece as he leaned down to stoke it. As the flames picked up the room seemed to be illuminated with slithering fingers making their way down from the ceiling. The smell of burning coal flowed into Matthias's nostrils and the mystic turned to face him.

"You can walk away from the fight. From the people who killed your sister. But the Legion will have won. There's no way you'd ever find Balthazar Nunez and certainly, without proper training, no way you could best him. But, you can walk away. Or you can stay. Learn. Prepare." The two men looked at each other and gave Mathias time to consider.

He already knew this was the answer. Now he had found a path to his revenge. One that would lead him to the man who killed Rebecca.

"I want to learn to fight," he said, "I want to join you."

"Yes," said Mr Hardy in a soft voice, "I believe you do. I also know how much you must be hurting at this moment. But I need you to understand something. The decision you now take upon yourself shouldn't be taken lightly. The road ahead of you is long and hard; most difficult."

"I understand," said Matthias, "but this is all there is for me now."

"Not so," replied Mr Hardy, "there are other places you could go. We could ensure your safety. Maybe even find a family who would take you in."

He thought about the offer. A family. But then his thoughts turned to his sister. His sister who would never know a family; who would never again run or play; who would never laugh, nor cry, nor sing, nor dance.

"Rebecca and the children at the abbey never received such an offer. It is in their name I must decline it."

Mr Hardy looked at Matthias once more with those big gentle eyes. A small smile creased the corner of his mouth.

"Very well," he said. "Report to the mustering hall at eight o'clock tomorrow morning. You can start basic hand to hand combat training. We'll see how you go from there. Mr O'Grady will be your instructor. Be courteous at all times and treat him with the utmost respect...if you want to end the day in one piece."

"Yes, sir."

"One more thing. We do not use surnames here you will be known only as Matthias. Is that clear?"

"Yes."

"People have to *earn* their family names, whatever it is." The smile had gone.

Matthias got up to leave but paused. "My grandfather," he asked, "will I get to meet him?"

"All in good time," said Mr Hardy, returning to his notes. As Matthias made his way slowly back to his room he found himself wondering what he had let himself in for.

Chapter 6

When Matthias awoke the next day Harry was already up and sitting on the end of his own bed reading a book. He was used to sharing a dorm with ten or twelve others, so to have just one companion was a first. The boy turned and looked at Matthias as he sat up and rubbed his eyes.

"You're awake then?" he said, in a jolly voice.

Matthias yawned and scratched his head. With so much going through his mind and his body shaking with cold he couldn't really focus on early morning conversation.

Harry stood up. "I said, 'You're awake then?'" His voice was accented and more common than the other children he had heard around the castle.

"I'd say so," said Matthias. He got up and hopped barefoot across the cold stone to the trunk at the end of his bed and started to dress. He took off his nightgown and placed it inside where the clothes he had arrived in lay. They looked sad, discarded at the bottom of the trunk. After changing into his new livery he took one last look at the white shirt and brown breeches before closing the lid.

"Are you to train with us then?" said Harry, starting to get ready himself. Matthias looked him squarely in the eye. The boy grinned back.

"Yes," said Matthias, "I am to learn to fight."

"Great," said Harry. "Who have they started you with? O'Grady I expect?"

Matthias nodded, whilst adjusting his new clothes. They fitted well and were thick and hard wearing. The fine materials clung to his frame tightly and the duke's emblem shone on his chest. At his side he hung a small dagger which had been provided with the garments.

"He's a tough one; be warned," continued Harry. "He'll start you off slow, but as soon as he sees that look in your eyes he'll want to find out what you're made of."

Matthias finished buckling his belt, "What *look*?"

Harry turned to face him fastening on a sword belt that held a foil neatly in place at his side. "Why, the look you're giving me right now. It may make you feel a bit stronger and give the world the impression you are trouble, but in here it'll just make people think you're scared. Some of the young 'uns try it. I hear they don't last long."

Harry took a step closer and whispered in his ear, "A word of advice. If you want to last, don't try and act as a hero. You won't fool anyone and you'll probably get your neck snapped."

He gave Matthias a friendly pat on the back and said, with an enormous grin, "Come on, it's in the morning hall. I'll take you there."

Matthias sighed and let his face relax from the distant stare and square jaw he realised he had been wearing and followed his roommate. As they walked he tried to remember the corridors they had come down as feeling sure he would get lost returning.

They eventually reached the hall and it was enormous. Along its walls hung all manner of weapons and armour. Different types of swords at one end, all neatly side by side – there must have been twenty or thirty of each type! Next to them were helmets, breastplates and further along a collection of wooden weapons.

It was near these were a group of perhaps twenty or thirty children gathered; all younger than Matthias, but not much. They were chatting idly amongst themselves. Matthias could see many of them had wooden swords on their belts and all had studded jackets of leather.

As Harry led them in, some of the children stared and looked him up and down. Matthias made his way to the back of the group and tried to avoid their looks.

The biggest of a group of three boys turned and said out loud, "Our new teacher looks a bit young!"

There were a few guffaws but thankfully most of the class ignored him. The boy poked his friend in the ribs and was just about to come out with another jibe when he received a sour look from Harry.

"He's with me, Walter," said Harry. He turned, gave Matthias a wink, and then left via one of the other corridors. The other boy turned back to his friends with a sideways look at Matthias.

Whilst they waited he started to take in more of the scene. Hanging on the other walls were ropes, climbing equipment and harnesses; then, further along, pistols and muskets. The majority of the hall was covered in a thick carpet the like of which Matthias had never seen; it almost made him bounce with each step.

As Matthias looked around the children he noticed they appeared agitated. Some were fidgeting with the straps on their armour and belts, others simply looking at the floor with gloom. He once again found himself squaring his jaw and setting his shoulders back. Today was all about learning he reminded himself. Pay attention, do exactly as the teacher says and treat him with respect.

For several more minutes they waited, the air getting tenser. Then, from a far door, a man marched in wearing a thick leather jerkin and trousers. His red face was accompanied by grey hair and an even greyer bushy beard making him look like a knight from the Crusades. He strode over purposefully to the group and barked at them like a general, "Alright everyone. Let's have you." The children all scurried to line up against the wall and Matthias fell in at the end. The barrel-chested teacher walked down the line looking at each child in turn until finally he came to Matthias.

"I'm Mr O'Grady, your instructor. Follow my instructions and try to keep up and I think we'll get along just fine." Up close the man was intimidating. His face had several scars that looked almost as old as him and his teeth were black and broken. A rapier hung at the side of his belt and his fingers danced across the hilt when he shouted. It looked as if he was about to draw it upon one of the children and Matthias wondered for a moment whether he ever had.

"Walter, Stephen, Raphael. Present!" he bellowed. The three boys who had been sniggering all leapt forward and drew their wooden swords before standing in a line. O'Grady walked up to the wall and took down two wooden swords, one of which he threw to Matthias without a word. He then took off his sword belt and handed his rapier to another student.

"En garde!" he yelled, and then advanced on the three boys. Immediately the three of them split up so as to encircle the instructor and the other children watched, fascinated. Then, like a snake pouncing, the first of them leapt at O'Grady without fear.

The boy's lunge seemed slow and clumsy, or maybe that was just the way O'Grady made it look as he easily flicked the low strike aside and countered with one to the boy's chest. The boy sunk to his knees in genuine pain from the strike but the instructor was not done yet. The old man swiftly followed up with another crack straight in the boy's ribs who finally collapsed.

O'Grady turned to face the other boys but addressed the groaning mass on the floor to his side. "Too easy, Stephen. Very slow, even for you. The strike was too low for a target taller than yourself. Get up!"

The boy groaned on the floor and Matthias thought he heard a faint, "Yes-sir," muffled into the carpet. Stephen got on to his knees rubbing his ribs and, with a sullen look, made his way back to the line taking deep breaths.

The two remaining boys shared a slightly nervous look with each other but maintained their calm and prepared to strike. First up was the one Harry had called Walter. He crept to within striking range of the teacher but merely carried out small thrusts well out of reach, presumably he was testing the range of the man.

"Come along Walter," said O'Grady. "Show me your mettle, boy."

Walter stepped back and to Matthias's surprise leapt straight at the teacher, only he went up and up; perhaps twenty feet over the instructor's head. O'Grady turned to face the boy who had landed behind him. "Good, Walter. But you'll get nowhere jumping around all day."

Matthias turned to look at his classmates; they were all staring intently. Nobody seemed to have notice the boy had leapt the height of a house! Mr Hardy had called the children 'gifted' and he was beginning to understand why.

The boy took barely a step back but leapt again and this time quickly turned and lunged. His strike looked true, but once more O'Grady was quicker, he knocked the boy's blade aside and thundered into him with his shoulder. The youngster's breath could be heard leaving his body as he too fell to the floor.

"Too open Walter! Were you paying attention last week? It's all about the footwork boy." He looked up at the remaining opponent who had now turned slightly pale.

The boy was quivering, his breathing quick as he tried to maintain his composure. He looked at the old instructor who stared back with mad eyes. Then, something seemed to snap within him and he lunged. It was clumsy even to a layman and the boy's sword was wild and high. O'Grady made it look simple when he ducked, disarmed and flung the boy over his shoulder. He landed heavily only a few feet from Matthias.

"Disappointing class," said O'Grady, re-adjusting his belt and jacket. "Clearly people haven't been paying attention. Right here we just saw three prime examples of what *not* to do. Never miscalculate your opponent's strengths, never go in open and always watch your feet. Balance is of the highest importance."

The class nodded glumly. Then O'Grady looked at Matthias. "You, new boy. What's your name?"

"Matthias, sir."

"Let's see what you're made of, come on. I'll go easy on you."

Matthias remembered he was gripping a wooden sword; though more out of fear than preparation. "Sir?"

"Come at me. I won't hurt you."

He gingerly stepped forward and held the sword at what he approximated was a fencing stance. "En garde!" bellowed the instructor. They immediately began to circle each other as the boys before had done. "Now remember what you've seen here," said O'Grady, "Keep your balance, attack high and don't open up your body."

Energy pulsed through Mathias as his arms, legs and even his stomach tightened. Somehow his fear had vanished and an animal instinct took over. Every muscle in his body burst into life and it was almost as if time slowed down around him. For a second he thought he saw a small look of confusion cross the instructor's face. He picked this as his moment to attack and leapt at him sideways with the wooden sword.

O'Grady instinctively brought up his own to block and disarm Matthias but he had been expecting this and had already planned his next move. The attack was a feint and he used his own motion to spin around the disarming move and turn his back to the teacher. He finally brought the sword up to the teacher's throat in a sharp thrust. There was silence as the class stood open-mouthed looking at the two in front of them. O'Grady with his arms by his side and Matthias standing in front him, back to chest but with the sword held above his head and poking into the man's throat.

"Impressive," smiled O'Grady. "I can see we'll have some fun." He started chuckling and Matthias thought he felt him press in closer to the sword.

"Only one thing." This time he definitely leaned in to the dull wooden point. "You're slightly off balance." With those words he whipped Matthias's legs out from underneath him.

He fell to the floor and landed with a thump on his back. Now O'Grady had the upper hand and he didn't waste a moment. Before Matthias could recover the older man had crossed his own two swords to make a 'V' around Matthias's neck. The crazed eyes glared down at him and the mouth formed a crooked, blackened grin.

"With a little hard work we can make sure you don't overstretch yourself, eh?" The teacher stood back and offered Matthias his hand before hoisting him up. Massaging his throat he took his place in line with the other boys and felt a touch of pride as he noticed a few of the looks of curiosity he had garnered.

The rest of the morning was spent concentrating on footwork through a combination of lectures and then more complex balancing exercises. Once Matthias got to grips with the theory it came naturally to him to be able to follow O'Grady's moves and steps. This soon became apparent to everyone and several of the other boys started to look at him with suspicion.

At midday they broke for lunch and Matthias followed the flow of children toward the smell of food coming from a banqueting hall. It was there the familiar face of Harry appeared bobbing through the crowds.

"Ahoy there!" he shouted. Matthias managed a smile and waved weakly. It had been an exhausting morning and he was looking forward to some food.

"How was the class?" said Harry.

"It was good," said Matthias, as they made their way to the queue of children receiving food. "I think I'm going to like it here."

"Oh really? I heard you gave O'Grady a few surprises."

As they reached the front of the queue they were handed an empty bowl each. This was promptly filled by a maid with a mixture of meat, vegetables and broth. Next to it was a large basket of bread and Matthias helped himself to three pieces.

"Everyone's saying you managed to beat his disarming move with your first attempt! I know you're a little older than the other children in the class but it's still impressive. I imagine they'll have you joining the rest of us within the week."

"I hope so. I want to learn as much as I can as quickly as I can." He took a tankard of water and followed Harry to a table. They both started eating; it was good food and he was glad of the bread to add substance to the meal. The banqueting hall bustled with what must have been close to a hundred children all eating and talking excitedly.

One of them approached the table. He was bigger and older, maybe eighteen, with blond hair and blue eyes that narrowed when he saw Matthias. "Hello Harry," he said with a big smile. "Who's your new friend?"

"Alexander, meet Matthias. Matthias, Alexander." Harry didn't even look up from his food.

"Matthias? An unusual name."

"He's from far away."

"Oh, I see. Anyway, I just thought if you wanted me to join you for lunch, I could perhaps sit here?"

"Not today, thanks."

The boy's smile dropped and he looked crestfallen as he walked away to an empty table. As he turned and walked away Matthias noted the other children seemed to ignore him too.

"Who was that?"

"That's Alexander," said Harry. "He's a bit of a strange one. Spends most of his time in the chapel. Doesn't really have many friends. I talk to him occasionally but only because I feel sorry for him."

Matthias watched as the boy drifted to an empty table at the edge of the room where he sat down to eat his meal alone before turning back to Harry.

"So what have you been doing today?" he asked, between mouthfuls.

"Ballistics."

Matthias looked puzzled.

"Shooting?" said Harry. "It's pretty easy once you get the hang of it…rather boring actually. But after you've completed your apprenticeship, that's when selection happens and you become a Journeyman."

"Journeyman?" Matthias realised in all his eagerness to take up arms he'd forgotten to ask any of the basic questions of how long he would be here and what exactly his training entailed.

"Yes, Journeyman," Harry took a swig of water from his tankard and wiped his mouth. "Everyone starts their apprenticeships first. Maybe half a dozen or so out of each class complete and then they get to become a Journeyman."

"You mean it's not like joining the army?"

Harry scoffed and returned to his bowl. "No, this is an academy. You have to pass all the tests for each discipline – swordsmanship, shooting, physiology, chemistry…"

"Physiology?" said Matthias.

"Yes," replied Harry, "The study of the body; I know, I'd never heard of it either."

"I don't understand. Why study the human body? I thought I was here to learn how to fight?"

"But you are," said Harry, "and for that you have to understand how the human body works. Where all the organs are; weak spots, veins and arteries. You need to know all this when you're making kills."

Matthias looked around. All the children were laughing and chatting away, each with a bowl of broth in front of them. He looked back at Harry who was finishing off his food and wiping the bowl with the bread. "I thought this was like the army?"

Harry looked at Matthias for a split second and then chuckled. "The army?" said Harry, holding another chuckle. "Who told you that?"

"Well, I just thought...Mr Hardy said I would be trained in combat. I thought this was, well, an army?"

Matthias suddenly felt very unsure of himself. What was the word Father James had used? *Assassins*. At the time he had pressed on with his questions about the Legion never asking for an explanation of the word. He hadn't wanted to admit he had never heard it before.

Harry looked at him and put the last of his bread in his mouth. He narrowed his eyes as if looking for something. "You really don't understand do you?"

He shook his head before Harry offered a smile. "Finish that and follow me." Matthias put the last piece of crust in his mouth and followed Harry out of the hall and up some stone stairs. They continued up several floors and then came to a wooden door. As they opened it Matthias was blasted by bright sunlight and blown almost off his feet by a strong wind. They were stood on the battlements of the castle.

Harry leaned over the high stone wall and looked down. Matthias did the same and started when he saw the ground far below. Harry put his arm out to help him back.

"I've never been this high before," snapped Matthias. He crept cautiously to the edge and again looked over. The sight was truly impressive. Below him was the great courtyard of the castle where children scurried around on their way to classes. Two coaches were arriving and further out, stretching all the way to the horizon were fields, farms and forest for as far as he could see.

The bright sun beat down but a harsh wind was also pounding them. Harry had to shout to be heard as he spoke. "This is just a small part of the duke's lands. Look around you!"

Again his eyes turned to the landscape. The fields swished violently as the wind hit them. Even the forest flickered and changed colour as gales sent the trees first one way and then the other.

Harry stepped close to Matthias and looked him in the eye. "Armies only fight other armies. Our war has no armies," he shouted.

"Then what are we doing here?" bellowed Matthias, the wind howling at his ears.

"All this is just basic training. Combat, fitness, biology, even etiquette classes for some. All training to separate the chaff from the wheat."

"So what happens to the wheat?"

Harry stood close next to Matthias and held his shoulders. "You'll be an assassin," he said, and offered a strange smirk.

"I don't know what this word means."

Harry looked confused and his eyes flickered as if something was finally registering. He nodded to himself.

"You'll be taught to kill and then be sent to kill. In secret, abroad or at home. In the houses of kings or the cottages of farmers. You'll usually not know them and you'll rarely know why. But you'll do it; without question, without hesitation."

Matthias's head rocked back. He knew a little about what an army was, how they worked and what they did. He had even imagined himself in battle but this was something different. The wind had died down now and the skies were darkening. Matthias was still getting buffeted though and he struggled to stay on his feet but he wasn't sure whether it was the wind causing this anymore.

"Do you understand now?" Harry said.

Matthias nodded weakly. Harry shouted, "Isn't it exciting?"

And then he started to laugh. Loud and heartily and long and hard. Matthias couldn't join in and just stood there as this boy laughed and laughed like some crazed clown. After a while they made their way back down the stairs in silence. At the bottom Harry informed Matthias that his next class was to be physiology and he gave him directions. As they turned and parted company, Matthias stopped and asked him one last thing. "Who do we kill?"

Harry looked at the floor for a moment and appeared to turn this question over in his head. "You never know until you're given the order. It could be a footman; it could be a lord or a lady. You just do it."

Matthias nodded slowly and looked down the long dark corridor ahead of him to the classroom. As he started to walk he heard Harry whisper, "After a while, I hear you start to enjoy it."

Chapter 7

The afternoon physiology lesson was with Mr Butler – a tall lean fellow who wore glasses and spoke in a quiet, raspy voice. He constantly asked the children to stop murmuring and pay attention but his soft whispers often got lost in the big echoing stone room they sat in.

Around them were skeletons hanging in display cases; on great shelves sat jars of specimens and vials of liquid. At the front Mr Butler was going through all the bones in the human hand using a chalkboard. Once again, Matthias was grouped with the younger children and he felt a little foolish as he answered some of the easier questions. That is, until they had to take a written test. To his embarrassment and the sniggers of others he repeated his answer to Mr Butler.

"I cannot write, sir," he said, looking down at the blank paper in front of him and the pen sat next to the jar of ink.

The teacher came to a halt in front of his wooden desk. As he spoke his soft face looked saddened. "My dear boy, have you ever been schooled at all?"

"No sir," said Matthias. "Only Bible lessons at the abbey."

Mr Butler's jet black eyes glistened with sadness. His slender features dropped slightly and he took Matthias gently by the arm.

"Come with me. We shall speak to Mr Hardy at once." Matthias got up and allowed himself to be led to the door. When they reached it Mr Butler turned to the class and said, "The rest of you may begin." As they left the room the last thing Matthias heard was the turning of papers and the furious scribbling of pens.

They made their way to Mr Hardy's office and Mr Butler wasted no time at all in knocking on the door and letting himself in. Mr Hardy was lost in papers at his desk but he looked up and raised an eyebrow after Mr Butler let loose an audible cough.

"Mr Butler. Matthias. How can I help you?"

"Mr Hardy, were you aware Matthias cannot read or write?"

Mr Hardy straightened in his chair, "Is this true?"

Matthias felt the need to correct, "I can read a little, sir. But… I cannot write."

Now Mr Butler turned to Matthias. "You can read, but not write?"

"Yes, sir. Father James taught us to read for Bible classes, but the abbey never had writing lessons."

The physiology master turned to Mr Hardy with a look of concern on his face. "Matthias will need to learn to write."

"Yes, but maybe this is something best handled by Lady Taylor? Matthias needs to be instructed in the ways of society much quicker than the other children."

Mr Butler raised an eyebrow and moved closer to the desk. "I don't follow."

Mr Hardy waved him away, "Never mind. We can discuss it later. For now we must ensure he is schooled in writing, literature, dance, conversation and etiquette." At the mention of the word 'dance' Matthias visibly stiffened.

The master stood up and closed the great book he had been writing in. "Mr Butler, I will arrange for Matthias to have writing lessons and will take up the other gaps in his knowledge with Lady Taylor. For now, can he take part in your lessons and perhaps carry out some sort of oral test?"

Mr Butler looked flustered - he was clearly not used to making exceptions. He played with his silk neck tie and looked at Matthias with disregard. "This is most irregular. What I teach cannot be learned by word of mouth alone. The Latin, the drawings…"

"I can take care of this. For now, please do the best you can with him. I will place him immediately into private tuition for his writing."

"Very well," said Mr Butler, "if you are sure you can find someone to undertake this task outside of academy hours?"

"I have just the fellow. Mr Butler, please return to your class and continue. I shall be in contact. Matthias, follow me." The master reached for his black velvet coat and escorted out Mr Butler who left looking perplexed. Mr Hardy turned and walked off in the opposite direction. After several paces he bellowed, "Do hurry up!"

For the second time Matthias was led out into the maze-like corridors. They walked for a short time to a part of the castle he had not yet been to - the chapel. It was instantly recognisable by the pews and candles, not to mention the giant crucifix hanging above the ornate stone altar.

It was strange to enter a church within a castle but when they passed through the rather humble doors they were instantly engulfed in a solemn quiet and the wind could be heard whispering around them. Mr Hardy's voice, however, cut through the calmness when he called out, "Father James!"

Matthias looked around the building which was enormous and was much bigger than the small chapel there had been at the abbey. Gold leaf decorated the vast walls and oil paintings depicted scenes from the Bible, not all of them pleasant. Wooden columns went all the way along to the altar at the front supporting a great arched ceiling; too high for Matthias to see the details of the coats of arms and crests that adorned it.

But dust and cobwebs obscured the grand furnishings and even the floor itself had a fine coating. Several sets of footsteps where visible but it was clearly not in use.

A shuffling behind them announced Father James arriving from a door at the back. He extended his arm out to Matthias and held his hand firmly with both of his. "My boy," he said, "how are you?"

"I am well, uncle. My first day has been interesting." Father James gave Mr Hardy a quizzical look but the Master of the Sandstone Castle simply raised an eyebrow.

"Matthias has never learnt to write. Is this correct?"

Father James scratched his white beard. "Why yes. But he can read, although it was never one of his great strengths."

"Did any of the children at the abbey learn to read or write?"

At the mention of the children Father James's face immediately darkened and looked distant. His eyes fell to the floor and he took hold of Matthias by the arm. "The children were raised in the countryside. They were to leave one day and work as farmers, labourers or, if they were lucky, artisans. They picked a craft, learnt basic reading and arithmetic if required and then they found work when they were old enough."

"I don't understand. Surely your father would have made some provision…"

Father James lifted his head slowly. "My father disagreed with my methods and with my faith."

Mr Hardy shook his head solemnly. "My apologies. I misspoke."

Father James nodded his head in forgiveness. Mr Hardy looked at Matthias and said, "James, it would be of a great service to us all, now that he has entered the academy, if he could be taught to read and write to a higher level. His opportunities and needs have changed."

"This can be done. It would please me to spend time with my nephew. The chapel here is filling the rest of my time. It has fallen into quite a state."

Mr Hardy turned to look around him. "It has been empty several years. But it is very kind of you to offer to maintain it on our behalf."

"Maintain it?" said Father James. "My dear sir, this is a house of God. I serve this place. I shall endeavour to bring it back to its former glory."

Mr Hardy tilted his face. "The wind of faith in the castle is an idle one and these children have no time for preparing to meet their maker. They leave it to the old." He started to walk away.

Father James spoke as he reached the door, "Some of these children won't get a chance to become old Mr Hardy."

The master paused and looking down he sighed. His head turned and Matthias thought he was about to speak, but instead he walked out through the dark archway in silence.

Father James waited a moment before gathering himself and turning to Matthias. "Come, let us begin your studies."

The old monk opened the wooden door at the back of the chapel through which he had emerged, his brown robes flapping as he walked, and they made their way down a dark and dingy corridor to a little room lit by a solitary candle.

It was a small and simple chamber with books in great piles on the shelves, floor and a table. A window was high on the far wall but the shadows on this side of the castle ensured very little sunlight got through.

A movement caught Mathias's eye and he realised they weren't alone. On the floor, scrubbing the stone, was Alexander. He immediately sat up, "Hello Matthias." The eyes shined in the dimness and he put down his scrubbing brush and dried his hands on his tabard.

"Alexander," said Father James. "What are you doing here?"

"Cleaning the floor. I spilt some ink and didn't want it trodden around."

The monk pulled out a chair and sat down slowly, watching Alexander. "I see you've met my nephew, Matthias. He's here to study so I'll need some time alone with him."

Alexander looked shocked. "Nephew?"

"Yes. I'll need some time alone with him. " His uncle did it subtly but Matthias noticed him signal toward the door. For a moment Alexander did nothing but stare and Matthias thought Father James was about to lose his temper.

Alexander finally nodded his understanding, but kept looking at Matthias with curious glances. Was it fear?

"I beg your pardon. I'll be out of your way now." He picked up his bucket and brush and darted away.

Father James started shuffling piles of papers and moved a stack of tomes to reveal two chairs and pulled them over. He moved a pile of dusty manuscripts and placed them carefully on the floor next to a desk under yet more shelves.

"A nice boy, but quite odd. Very pious though, which can only be a good thing. Apparently he's been looking after this place all by himself." His uncle smiled and gestured to a seat.

"What is all this?" asked Matthias.

"The previous occupant," said his uncle, "Father Morant, so Alexander tells me. This was his life's work. Histories, notes, works of literature; some of them hundreds of years old. All left here and forgotten about. I've been looking through them, attempting to bring some order to the chaos. He was a fascinating man."

Matthias picked up a well-worn book next to him whose title was *A Historie of the Founteyn*. On the front carved in leather was the now familiar duke's emblem. "What happened to him?" he asked.

Father James lifted his head up from behind a box of papers. "I've made some enquiries but nobody seems to know. They say he left many years ago. Though quite why is unknown. In any case he left all this here. It's interesting what I've read so far. Maybe we could use some in your studies? Bring your reading up to scratch?"

"I would like that," said Matthias, returning the tome to the table.

They spent the rest of the afternoon practising reading and he was surprised at how much he could remember. The alphabet all fell into place and he managed to read a whole chapter from a book of Bible stories although he did need some help with the odd word and some of the longer place names. The lack of sunlight didn't help but his uncle seemed so happy in his little room surrounded by books that he thought it would be unfair to ask could they move. Besides, it felt good to be around a familiar face and he could recognised the feeling in his uncle too.

As the sunlight all but disappeared somewhere in the castle a bell struck seven. Father James looked up from the volume they had been reading together. "I believe a meal will be served now. Come, I'll take you to the mustering hall."

"You know the way?" said Matthias, stretching as he got up; the old wooden stool he had been sat on was far from comfortable.

"Of course," said Father James, "I spent four years here myself."

Matthias halted, "What?"

His uncle frowned. "I trained here for four years at my father's wishes. A long, long time ago." He sighed. "It didn't suit me. I chose to follow the path of our Lord."

They started to walk back out to the chapel. In the corridor it was near total blackness and Matthias had to hold his hand out to the walls to make sure he didn't lose his way.

"It was a dark time for me," continued the monk. "I was lost in this place. These walls were my prison. I didn't belong here."

They entered the chapel and Father James turned to him. "I chose a different life than your father. But it was a choice Matthias, nevertheless. You have that choice too. Do you understand what I'm saying?"

"Yes," he replied. "I have chosen."

His uncle rested his arms on his shoulders. "You will learn in time it becomes very hard to change the mould of your life. The choices you make here, the actions you carry out beyond these walls; doubt me not, will touch your very soul."

They continued in silence to the hall and Matthias sat down next to Harry who was on his own. Father James went off to another table to sit with some teachers.

Harry turned to him and said, "How was physiology then?"

Mathias looked down at his plate. "It went well," he lied.

Harry started to eat his supper of soup, cold meat and bread. "Not what I heard," he said, "rumour is that you can't read." He turned to look at Mathias with a hint of a smile on his face. Mathias exhaled and took a piece of bread. It seemed the rumour mill at the castle was constantly one step behind him.

All around children talked and ate. The air was bursting with the sounds of people filling their stomachs. But to Matthias there was only his own very heavy silence.

"Don't worry about it," said Harry, "I can help." He gave him a friendly pat on the arm. "You'll need some help with drawing too I would imagine. Mr Butler makes you copy out pictures of organs and limbs."

Matthias, his face red, looked at Harry with a weak smile. "Thank you."

"Oh how sweet," said a new voice. The two boys turned to look at its owner. Sitting opposite them, where seconds ago there had been an empty space, was Sophie. She smirked and her eyes drooped in mock sadness. "You two boys must be the 'bestest' of friends now?"

"Very funny, Sophie," said Harry and as he brought his spoon of soup up to his mouth he flicked it straight at her. The murky brown liquid splashed onto her black tunic but it was quickly absorbed.

"How juvenile!" Sophie looked at Harry with disdain and dabbed at her clothing. She turned to Matthias and he had his first chance to look at her properly.

She was pretty with pale white skin, a round face and deep brown eyes. Her shiny, jet black hair framed her features before falling smartly to her shoulders . She spoke with breeding but then, she was the daughter of a lord, Mathias recalled. Or was it a baron? Matthias couldn't remember exactly but felt sure she would see herself as his better.

"I heard you excelled at hand to hand combat. You boys are always so rough." She began eating and studying some notes at the same time.

"Do you learn combat?" Matthias asked.

Sophie looked up from her notes in something approaching disgust. "Combat?" she choked, "Heavens no. I'm preparing to specialise my skills and become a Journeyman."

"In what?" said Matthias, mopping up the last of his supper with a piece of crusty bread.

"Poisoning," said Sophie, and with a delicious smile she stared at the piece of bread half way towards Matthias's mouth. He stopped an inch short, his mouth wide open. His gaze fell to the soggy bread in his fingers and then back to Sophie's dark brown eyes as they stared at it.

She chuckled and then both her and Harry started to laugh. Harry spoke first, "Don't worry, your supper is quite safe."

"You really don't understand how this place works, do you?" said Sophie.

"I'm getting the hang of it," said Matthias, placing the bread back on his plate. "So how long before you're a Journeyman?"

"Next spring. I'll finish advanced training and complete a thesis on poisoning. They say within a year I'll be ready for my first assignment."

"And what do you say?" said Matthias.

"I say you can never truly learn anything. I'm only just scratching the surface. There are so many wonderful plants and creatures in this world that the number of toxins documented barely constitutes a fraction. One day, I'd like to travel far away and bring back something new. Something special."

"How long does training take? When will I get to pick something?"

"It's different with each person," said Harry. "For Sophie here it'll be two years in spring. Most are usually more than that."

Matthias felt himself deflate a little. Two years? He had a long road ahead. Still, he could learn. He could become strong and he could avenge his sister. At this thought he once more felt a surge through his body and his mind clear. There was an energy inside him now, a punishment ready to be delivered. It felt good and he knew he could draw on it when he needed. He wouldn't let her down.

They finished their meals and headed back to their rooms. Matthias and Harry lit a candle and talked away briefly before sleep. Matthias learnt that Harry had been brought up in a village in Hampshire. After being found abandoned, a local couple had taken him onto their farm. When his stepmother had died and his stepfather became ill Harry had taken to poaching from the local lord's estate. The only trouble was that with his skill at staying hidden and blending in with his surroundings he became too good at it.

Stories started to circulate the village about a strange beast that was slaying the local deer and rabbits. Of course, Harry knew better, but the villagers had reacted one night and sent out a party to search the woods. They'd caught Harry red-handed with a stag and half a dozen rabbits in a makeshift smoker he'd built. Threatened with being sent away to the navy he had taken the offer to come to the castle from the mysterious Spanish mystic Alonso who had turned up shortly after his misadventure.

Matthias felt glad there was someone here who was also an outsider like him. He shared some of his own story but left out the part about the attack on the abbey. He wasn't yet ready to relive those events for anyone. He had kept his feelings hidden inside and they would remain there until he was ready to unleash his anger on the man who had killed Rebecca.

Chapter 8

The next day Matthias awoke early. The mustering hall was just coming to life and a few children were sitting down at the tables. Bleary eyed as they were, there was little chatter to be heard and Matthias found himself wondering how tough his day was going to be. He felt more confident now he had his reading and writing arranged with his uncle but today still held some trepidation for him. He was to begin ballistics lessons with Major Wilson.

Harry had told him about the gruff, old officer who had fought at Waterloo before taking up a post at the academy. Even though Matthias had scant knowledge of history he found himself already in awe of the man as he made his way to the lesson after breakfast. He followed his classmates to the fields outside of the castle. There, a dozen or so students were in a line some one hundred yards away from straw targets. Major Wilson was nowhere to be seen and the children started to laugh and joke whilst they waited for his arrival.

Though the other children were relaxed, some had even brought pistols they were showing off, Matthias had to admit he was somewhat daunted at the thought of firing a gun. A familiar face smiled at him as he approached and Alexander struck up a conversation.

"Don't worry," he said, "he's not too bad. Rather strict, but fair."

"Harry tells me he can be tough on people who don't pay attention," replied Matthias, "but I guess that's because the guns are so dangerous."

Alexander smiled, "The major has always had a short temper; even at Waterloo he got up Wellington's nose. How are you finding it?" Alexander's soft blue eyes glistened and he tilted his head with genuine concern.

"I'm enjoying it," said Matthias. The boy's gentle nature seemed out of place amongst the other children; it was no surprise Matthias had heard some of them making fun of him. That must be why he spent most of his time in the chapel, away from their jibes.

He was just about to ask Alexander about his story when both of them jumped as a shrill voice snapped, "Attention children!"

An impressive man strode into view with an unmistakable military bearing. As he marched towards them carrying a great wooden case the students shuffled into a makeshift line. Immediately, however, his disdain became apparent, "What is this rabble?"

He was tall and built like an oak tree. He had short dark hair pressed tightly against his head and bushy whiskers sat proudly on his face turning his mouth into a permanent frown.

A boy named George started to speak but was immediately shouted down by the major. "You'll speak when you're spoken to, boy!" he roared, before dealing him a clip around the ear. The man strode along the line inspecting each and every one of them down his nose, until finally he reached Matthias and paused.

"Who are you?" he boomed.

"Matthias, sir."

"And to what do I owe the pleasure of you in my class?"

"Mr Hardy, sir," responded Matthias still staring at the floor. "I've just arrived at the castle and began my training. I'm new." He raised his head to catch a glimpse of the man's war-worn face. It was rough looking with a strong jaw. The eyes seemed to have a life of their own however and darted about frantically as he spoke.

"Very well," he said, before turning to his case. He reached inside pulling out a large gun which he held aloft. "Can anyone tell me what this is?"

Perhaps it was nerves, or a willingness to attain some credibility but Matthias spoke. "A musket?" Next to him, Alexander gave a hissing sound through his teeth.

"Musket?" The major's face erupted into a vision of horror, "Musket? This is a rifle boy, don't you know anything? One lap around the castle, now!"

He looked across at Alexander who gave a small smile of support before nodding to the castle. Slowly, and with a heavy head, Matthias set off. The castle itself wasn't too imposing, but because of its location at the top of a steep and well protected hill he had to run around the much larger base of the fortification itself. It took him about twenty minutes and when he got back the major had already distributed some rifles and set up a line of children. He pointed Matthias in the direction of an unattended weapon at the end.

The other children were already busying themselves with their equipment. The major decided to come over and give Matthias some individual tuition. "Alright lad, well done. Now, have you ever fired a gun before?"

"No sir," he said.

"Not to worry, nothing to it. Now, watch me." The man took the rifle in his hands and stood it upright, against his thigh. "Firstly, set the hammer to 'half cock', you don't want it going off whilst you're loading. Like so." He pulled back the claw like hammer until it gave a solitary click.

"Next, your charge," he said, producing a small paper ball-like object from the pouch on the floor. To Matthias's surprise he placed it in his mouth and bit off the end, "Place it in the barrel and put the ball on top. See?"

With interest Matthias noted that he hadn't in fact bitten off the top but merely separated a metal ball that was on top of the charge which he could only assume was the gunpowder.

"Put your wadding in here, set the rest of the charge, and then take your ramrod." The major pulled the metal rod from underneath the rifle's barrel as if he were drawing a foil, before lining it up with the opening and forcing it down with vigour three times.

"Finally, a spot of powder to the flash pan," he poured more gunpowder from a metal holder into a space underneath the hammer, "and she's ready!" He thrust the rifle into Matthias's arms and chest nearly knocking him off his feet.

His fingers found the trigger and he held the grip underneath the barrel as he could see the other children doing and aimed at the wooden targets further into the field.

"Now remember, hold your breath, count to three and squeeze the trigger! George?"

"Sir?"

"What do we do with the trigger?"

"Squeeze, sir!"

"Good, don't think I can't tell when you're not paying attention. Ready!"

It was not a question but a command and was swiftly followed with another, "Aim!" Matthias held the rifle tight to his chest. Not knowing what to expect he concentrated on keeping the heavy firearm level and pointed at his target. He held his breath and counted to three.

"Fire!"

The explosion hit Matthias's shoulder like a lead hammer, the noise deafened him and finally the powder in the flash pan blinded him. He dropped the rifle and started rubbing his eyes in pain, he was pretty sure he could smell burning hair too.

"What the blazes?"

Matthias could hear an exasperated Major Wilson but he couldn't see him.

"That's no way to treat a rifle! Two laps of the castle, I'll teach you drop my guns!"

Matthias, still rubbing his eyes, could make out the blurred shadow of the castle and started to stumble forward. He was helped by the major's boot connecting with his backside, much to the delight of the rest of the class who broke out in laughter. As he made his way up the path that lead around the craggy hill he heard Mr Wilson beginning to scold them. The lesson had only just begun and already he was desperate for it to end.

The rest of the afternoon didn't go much better; in all he managed to fire his rifle eight times, hitting the target not once. He did hit someone else's target and he also managed to make the entire class dive for cover when he turned to face the major with a question whilst still holding the rifle. That mistake had cost him four laps around the castle and then another two more for hitting Alexander's target who tried to show him some encouragement but in the end had had to admit Matthias was no marksman.

When he returned to his room he shared his afternoon with Harry who hooted with amusement. "I'm not particularly good at it myself," he said, whilst cleaning his boots, "but you sound dreadful. Remind me not to stand anywhere near you the next time you have a loaded gun!"

Matthias groaned as he sat down on the end of his bed, picked up his boots and started to clean. He had been told that the children were expected to be presentable at all times. This included polishing boots, buttons, belt buckles and also the daggers they each wore around their waist. Tonight was a formal supper, so it was even more important. Matthias would rather have just had some bread and milk and eaten in his room, but the castle was run like the military and ceremony seemed to be ever-present.

At supper he was placed next to Harry but the two boys, along with everyone else, had to remain standing until all the teachers had entered and seated themselves. In they walked one by one; Mr Butler who had led the physiology lesson; Mr O'Grady sauntered in and settled himself with a thud; Major Wilson and a couple more Matthias didn't recognise made up the rest of the table until finally Mr Hardy arrived at the head. He remained stood for some moments before finally calling out to the hall, "You may sit."

The scrapes of chairs and benches made the master wince as the children all sat down themselves. It was the first time Matthias had seen the whole academy together and he estimated there were nearly a hundred children, some younger than him, others older. Supper was served and everyone tucked in to potatoes and meat, served in a rich broth. It was delicious and Matthias finished his within minutes whereupon he sat back and gave a belch, which raised a chuckle from Harry.

They finished up with a pudding and then went back to their dormitory and both made straight for bed. After blowing the candle out Harry wished Matthias 'goodnight' before the sound of his light snores rumbled in the background. Once again, Matthias lay awake pondering his new life.

The place got stranger and stranger and he had to keep reminding himself why he was here. True, it was exciting – the combat, the ballistics (even though he was terrible), the exercises and other lessons still to come. It was all a new and wonderful world. But it had been hard so far, today especially. There was no doubt physically he was up to the task. He had already been able to measure himself against the other children and even though some of them were quick and strong he always felt one step ahead.

That feeling he got inside, almost a permanent inkling of what was about to happen. He had had it all his life but in this place it surged within him in everything he did. Maybe it was the very castle itself; maybe there was something special about it - precisely what though, he was still not fully sure.

Their customs and procedures seemed foreign to him and he spoke in a clumsy and common manner that none of the other children shared apart from Harry. Indeed at one point a couple of boys had looked to Sophie to translate when he had asked them where they were from. She had gladly assisted and the conversation had continued, but not without Matthias feeling awkward for the remainder.

That night he found himself roaming the castle, but it was empty. There were no other children and no teachers but in the great mustering hall he came across tables fully laden with food and crockery.

Then, a whisper. He wasn't alone after all, someone was there and they were laughing. He ran outside to the courtyard, but still the cackling voice in the darkness followed. Further and faster he ran around the castle through great halls and chambers, past tapestries and paintings but he could still hear the echoing laughter. No matter how hard he ran he couldn't get away nor could he turn to face his tormentor. Finally, cornered in a dungeon, his back to the wall he turned to face the shadowy figure.

In the darkness all he could make out was a great cape, or was it wings? The black silhouette stepped forward and lifted its arms above him. All was black except the flash of white teeth. Was it a grin or was it opening its mouth? With a scream of delight and a surge that lifted him up into the air the creature fell upon him and began to devour his flesh.

He woke up in a cold sweat out of breath and glad to see daylight. A concerned Harry was leaning over him, "Are you alright? You were screaming."

Matthias took some moments to compose himself before he sat up and rubbed his eyes. "I had a bad dream. Something was chasing me."

Harry gave a weak smile, "I know. It happens to a lot of us; it happened to me, at first. Once you get used to the place you'll be alright."

Matthias got up and made his way to the washbasin and splashed ice cold water on his face. Shaking his head he reached for his clothes and started to get dressed. On went his jerkin and belt along with the dagger. He touched it at his side and somehow got comfort from it. Picking up the papers Mr Hardy had given him with his lesson plans he looked at the calendar which dictated his week.

"What's 'Concealment'?" he said.

Harry span around from the washbasin with a grin. "That's my speciality. The art of hiding yourself from your enemy. You'll have Mr Fraiser. Expect to get dirty, you'll be out in the forest first lesson I imagine."

"In the forest?"

"Yes," said Harry, "You'll begin with simple covers and hides. Then maybe he'll have you in the mud and leaves and carrying out some training exercises."

"Mud and leaves?"

"It's a lot more fun than it sounds."

Chapter 9

It took Matthias several weeks to really settle down at the castle. For many nights sleep did not come naturally and more of his dreams were frightening and confused. Dark thoughts of death and violence would criss-cross his mind in nightmarish images. Sometimes he would see the faces of children he knew from the abbey. Sometimes he heard their screams and it was always late at night before he finally drifted away into some form of sleep.

The days, however, were progressing well. He had improved at combat and had heard mutterings from Harry that perhaps he was to be finally moved up to the senior classes. This came as a relief to him as he was older and taller than his classmates and sometimes felt embarrassed at the ease with which he dispatched opponents in fencing, his personal favourite.

However, not all of his peers were at a disadvantage. Quite quickly, he got to learn of the other children who possessed out of the ordinary abilities. Several could leap as high as a rooftop, others like Gerard had the strength of ten men. Indeed, in one unsavoury encounter in the courtyard the bully had upturned a local farmer's cart with one hand just to show off.

Being bigger, quicker and stronger however held no benefits in Mr Butler's physiology lessons. With help from his uncle Matthias had been learning to write and had also been practising his reading. The soft-spoken teacher had been kind enough to let him take some of the tests after class in the form of questions and drawings on the board. However, he had struggled. His brain had been unable to retain the scientific language or Latin and without the use of notes to read from it became even harder.

But Matthias found he had tremendous self-discipline and every night after dinner he spent time with his uncle reading and writing in the little study. Afterwards he'd try and fit some time in with Harry, if he wasn't busy with his own work, and practise drawing. The sketches came easily and he was surprised at how well he had been able to draw the organs that had been handed out in jars. Matthias had received a commendation for his picture of a heart, but was sadly let down by his labelling of the various parts which he couldn't remember even after Mr Butler had made him copy them down ten times.

The castle itself had seemed to change around him as the summer drew to a close. More and more lanterns and candles went up as the days grew shorter. Extra blankets had been delivered to his room along with a thick black cloak which, as with all of his clothes now, was adorned with the duke's emblem. They trained and learned every day except Sundays, which the children had to themselves. Most would go off in search of fun and adventure in the local village or forest but Matthias often went with Harry on walks and the two had become genuine friends.

Every Sunday morning Matthias would attend mass with Father James. It seemed strange the two of them all on their own in the great chapel sitting down to offer prayers and thanks, even taking communion. But to Father James, making sure the chapel was up and running seemed to tie in with his need for being useful. The old chapel and the old man gave each other a purpose.

It was on one such morning that Matthias joined Harry for a walk around the castle grounds. They had wandered a great circle around the orchard and gardens and were just about to turn into the courtyard when they noticed a rider heading up to the gates. Not unusual, but this person was with an armed escort. Four soldiers followed behind as the stranger made his way to the great wooden doors.

"I wonder who that is?" said Harry, tilting back his head. The two upped their pace as they reached the courtyard.

As they drew close they spotted the familiar livery of the duke on the soldiers' chests. The uniforms were bright blue and each man carried a sword and rifle. The horses were powerful specimens and as they dismounted and organised their packs in the courtyard the two managed to catch a glimpse of the stranger who led them.

A gallant, muscular man dressed in fine gentleman's clothes that hung on his frame, highlighting his physique. He brushed idly at his black riding boots and started to remove his saddle from the horse. He turned and smiled at them and from underneath his hat Matthias saw straight long red hair. His eyes were a pale green and his face was freckled and pale. He smiled and spoke, "Boys, would you inform Mr Hardy that Mr Cook has arrived?"

"Yes sir," said Harry, and the two headed off to fetch the master. They didn't need to go far however as they nearly ran into him turning the corner of the corridor to his office.

"Mr Cook has arrived, sir. He said to inform you."

Mr Hardy smiled. "Excellent. Did he have any men with him?"

"Four, sir," said Matthias.

"Follow me. You can help with the horses."

They walked back to the courtyard and the two gentlemen greeted each other like old friends. Servants were sent for to see to the men's baggage and Mr Hardy introduced Harry and Matthias as two promising students.

"Good to hear it," said Mr Cook. "I'm glad there's such talent coming through the ranks."

"Thank you," said Matthias, feeling more than a little awkward. He had still not received any of his social training from Lady Taylor, whom he had yet to meet. But he managed to hold his own in polite company and so far, he hoped, he hadn't offended anyone.

Mr Hardy cast Matthias a quick glance before saying, "Matthias is Michael's son."

Mr Cook's eyes opened wide immediately, "A good man and a good friend. You were at the abbey?"

"Yes, sir." Matthias noticed the curiosity on Harry's face.

"Alonso happened to have been in the area at the time," said Mr Hardy.

Mr Cook smiled, "Alonso is still searching for a special child?"

"You know Alonso. He is away following up some information we had on the episode. We believe it was Balthazar."

Mr Cook looked grave, "I thought he was in hiding?"

"We thought so too," said Mr Hardy, and there was a brief silence. "Come, let us get you refreshed. We have much to discuss and these boys need to get your horses to the stables and then I'm sure they have some work to do." The look Mr Hardy shot them implied that if they didn't he would find some for them. Both boys took their leave and went over to the horses.

"He knew my father. Who do you think he is? Surely not a teacher."

Harry started to gather the reins of the three nearest beasts; all fine stallions. "Don't know. But four soldiers? He must be pretty important."

"I wonder what he meant about a special child." Matthias, less confidently, pulled at the reins of the remaining pair. They didn't look like they wanted to move and the two horses started to inspect the floor with interest.

"Alonso?" said Harry, "They say he's looking for a special child or is it a cursed child? I can never remember; I think Mr Hardy humours him."

"Humours him?" Matthias tugged again at the reins and the horses reluctantly fell into line behind Harry and the others.

Harry turned and spoke over his shoulder. "Alonso is very superstitious. All mystics are. Don't you know much about them?"

It occurred to Matthias that he hadn't really given much consideration to the strange Spaniard who had found him that night near the abbey. "No," he said, "I've never met one of his kind before."

They walked on around the back of the castle to the stable entrance. Harry looked around, but the yard was empty.

"They come from the highest mountains. Life is hard and cruel up there but the mystics have learnt to adapt. They're big, strong and fierce fighters. But they can also see things we can't even begin to understand."

"What kind of things?"

"Nobody really knows. Some say the future. Others say they get visions. I asked him when he found me and he told me something I'm never to repeat."

"What?"

Harry snorted, "I can't say. But what he told me sent fear all the way to my stomach. He said I could never tell anyone. But I'll tell you this. He knows things. Things we don't."

He looked at Harry. The boy's face was deadpan. There was no hint of a smile or trace of sarcasm. "You're being funny."

"Not at all," said Harry. "You should learn to take me seriously when you need to."

The stable master, a stern looking man who surveyed them with suspicion, approached to take the horses before disappearing into the colossal stables.

Matthias turned and started to walk back. "I never know when that is, Harry. Come on, we'll be late." Both boys returned to their room and changed into their evening clothes for dinner. As they made their way there they ran into Sophie. She was carrying a large basket and seemed to be struggling.

"Let me help you," said Harry.

She gratefully shared the burden with him and offered her thanks. "Such a gentleman," she said. Matthias took the other handle of the large basket.

"Where have you been?" he asked.

Sophie started to adjust her dress and took a handkerchief out of a pocket, "Just to the forest, picking specimens."

Harry turned to Matthias with a questioning look. "Plants?"

"Why yes!" said Sophie. "I found some particularly good examples of long-leafed blackroot bulbs."

The pair followed the girl to her chamber with the basket. "I'm guessing these bulbs aren't particularly good for you?"

"Why, Matthias," she said, "the bulbs are harmless. True they are not edible but they will not kill you."

They arrived and two boys stopped to stare at the room. It which was much like their own except it was full of plants, jars, potions and pots. There was barely space for a bed but they found it and heaved the basket on top. She didn't share her quarters it seemed, though this was not surprising. Matthias guessed there would most likely be none willing to sleep and live in her room. She tended to distrust people, and they tended to offer the same sentiment back.

Matthias peered inside the basket and sure enough spotted lots of brown bulbs, each one as big as an apple, amongst other plants and leaves. He picked one up and smelt it but it was odourless. Harry too started to look inside and produced a handful of bright red grass.

"If it's not poisonous then why do you want it?"

"The bulbs aren't poisonous," said Sophie, "but if you boil them and then distil their juices, add a few other herbs, mix with a little yeast and vinegar then you have something that, for all intents and purposes, looks and tastes like mustard."

Matthias looked at Sophie with a barely concealed smile. "I'm guessing it's not mustard though." Sophie shook her head softly.

"What does it do?" said Harry.

Sophie played absentmindedly with a little blue plant that sat on her desk. "It makes your lungs bleed until you drown."

Matthias felt his jaw slowly fall and he put the bulb back in the basket. He turned to Harry who was looking equally appalled.

They chatted for a while; Sophie explaining about some of the other plants she had gathered and even letting them look at her collection of poisons kept under lock and key in a trunk under her bed.

Afterward, they made their way to the dinner hall in silence. Both Harry and Matthias were quietly contemplating the images in their heads that Sophie had inadvertently put there. Truth be told, Matthias found it all quite creepy. He had yet to really consider the thought that one day he may be ordered to kill someone or indeed take it upon himself to do so.

Meals on Sunday were a formal affair and took place in the dinner hall; a great room in the very centre of the castle. Shields, armour and various trophies of battles adorned the immense walls and large rectangular tables seated the students. The various tutors sat on their own up at the front atop a plinth with two great chairs at the back of them – Harry had explained these were for guests of honour or the duke.

The duke himself had yet to set foot in the castle. Matthias had asked his uncle many questions about him but the old monk seemed reluctant to talk about his father. In the end he had gathered as much information as he could from other students and even snippets from Mr Hardy. Matthias learnt that his grandfather rarely visited and spent most of his time in London. The castle was set aside purely as a training facility and not many even knew of its existence. The duke was now an old man but he was still wise and sharp and he was never seen without his personal guard.

After dinner he decided he was going to ask Mr Hardy if he had news of the duke's next visit. He was desperate to meet his grandfather, although he had told nobody else yet of this secret under strict instructions from the master himself.

As they ate Sophie and Harry picked up the conversation about the new arrival Mr Cook. Matthias listened but watched across the room as Mr Butler and then Mr Hardy chatted with him. Even toughened old O'Grady seemed to be a friend but the beautiful lady on the end of the table dressed in fine evening clothes was unknown to Matthias. A great blond wig over a foot high sat atop her soft and gentle face and he felt a tingle through his chest as her big dark brown eyes momentarily met his. She too seemed familiar with Mr Cook and smiled at his every word. Occasionally, with a fork, she would pick a little at her food and cast her eyes over the flame haired gentleman.

"Her, I don't know," said Matthias. "Another new arrival?"

"That's Lady Taylor," said Harry, with an ever so slight sigh. "She teaches etiquette and literature but doesn't live in the castle."

Sophie scoffed, "Harry's in love."

Harry's eyes flashed as he turned to face Sophie. "Am not," he said, but the damage was done and Matthias let a smile escape.

"I think you've got competition Harry," said Sophie, "she only has eyes for Mr Cook."

Harry's lips closed tightly together and his cheeks went red. Matthias decided to change the subject after receiving a wink from Sophie.

"So that's her. I don't understand why I am to be taught writing and manners though if I am to be a trained killer."

Sophie looked up from a book she had been reading; she always brought one to formal dinners which she found tiresome.

"To blend into society, Matthias, you need to know the rules."

"But why?" he asked.

"Because you're not a soldier," she said, closing the book with a snap. "You will have to slip into people's homes. Their lives. Their families even, to carry out your mission. We are trained to go were others cannot go and to do what others cannot do."

Harry was munching on some roast chicken and nodded. "She's right. Suppose you had to kill an earl or a duke? They're not going to let Matthias the dung farmer in to their private chambers now are they? And even if they did you'd never escape."

"Our missions are about secrecy. The idea is to get in and out without anyone ever suspecting it was you," finished Sophie, before returning to her book. She always seemed so very serious when talking about what lay on the various roads ahead.

Matthias finished the rest of his meal with these thoughts turning in his head. He realised he was going to need more time to adjust but, as always, he took strength from his thirst for revenge. It was a force inside him he could now summon at will. He was here and he had made a choice; a commitment which he was going to see to the end.

As they left the dinner hall he spotted Mr Hardy bidding farewell to Mr Cook and crossed the hall to enquire about his grandfather.

The master looked intrigued. "I think when his grace next honours us with his presence you will no doubt be presented to him."

"Thank you," said Matthias, unable to conceal his excitement. "That would be most - Thank you, sir!"

Mr Hardy went on, "He has personally expressed an interest in meeting you. After all, it was a great surprise for him to learn you had decided to join us."

Matthias blinked, "I see"

The master regarded him curiously, "Your uncle has not spoken to your grandfather for over twenty years. You are aware both your father and uncle didn't want you to come here?"

"Yes," he said.

"His Grace was most excited to learn you were to follow in your father's footsteps, but I fear this has only served to strengthen the divide."

Matthias decided to speak to his uncle at once. He found him, as usual, hunched over the great memoirs and volumes of the mysterious Father Morant.

"Matthias," he said, grinning warmly.

"My father really didn't want me here, did he?" As Matthias dumped himself on a stool at the desk the old monk's face changed to a serious expression and he frowned as he put down the book.

"It was your grandfather who delivered you and Rebecca to me that night many years ago. Your mother and father had been living in the country when you were born. They had decided to keep your existence secret until the time was right."

"The time was right?" said Matthias.

"These were troubled years. Your father and several agents had dealt a major blow to the Legion's forces. But they had struck back. Many battles were fought and lives lost."

"Was Mr Cook one such friend?"

"William is here?" said James. "Heavens, I haven't seen him in years. He and your father were very close."

"I feel like I know so little, yet everyone knows so much."

"Patience, Matthias," said his uncle, placing an arm around him. "Sometimes you must take a step back before you can walk forward."

The two sat in silence for some time. The dust falling on the old books caught the setting sun and twinkled in the air like sparks from a bonfire.

"Why did you let them take me in if my father never wished it?"

His uncle sighed and held him by the hand. "I felt it was time for you to start making your own choices. Truth be told, I saw your father's spirit in you. But also, a lack of discipline. If you had left the abbey to take up an apprenticeship I'll wager you would have found yourself in trouble soon enough. No doubt bored by the day to day plod of an honest labourer or smithy.

"This place has its faults. But it can teach you a great deal. Here you will learn not only dark skills, but useful ones too. They will make a gentleman of you, Matthias. Something I cannot do but something you deserve. Your grandfather will no doubt be pleased."

With these last words his uncle turned away but not before Matthias had seen him frown.

"They will change you. They will try to mould you. But who you are and what you choose to do after your education is entirely up to you. You could walk away. I'm you're your grandfather will be able to give you some land and an allowance. Or you could take the next step down the other path. A path of blood and death. I want you to have every chance to make the right choice. Your father felt that to do that you should be hidden. Well, there is nowhere to hide anymore, is there?"

His uncle squeezed his hand and gave him a warm hug. Both, though the other didn't know it, were thinking back to happier days at the abbey. Late summer afternoons in the orchard, children playing and the sound of laughter and games.

Chapter 10

The next day an animated Harry caught up with Matthias after a long morning with O'Grady. His muscles hurt and he'd caught a blow to the head off a young girl when he hadn't been paying attention.

"So why the excitement?" he asked, as they made their way to their dorm.

"Apparently there's a duelling contest tomorrow!"

As they walked into their small, shared room Matthias wasted no time in taking off his sweat soaked shirt and applying some ointment to his head. "Why the rush to get yourself killed?" he asked.

"We'll be using fake blades, idiot."

Matthias dabbed at the gash on his head and it smarted where a 'fake' blade had caught him hours earlier. He vowed to get his own back on that little ginger haired girl the next time he had O'Grady's class. They were supposed to practice defensive strokes but there was nothing defensive about the way she'd clobbered him.

"What's this?" said Harry, pointing at a comb.

"I have my first lesson with Lady Taylor today. I was told I have to look smart."

"Good luck!" said Harry, as he grabbed his cloak to leave. "It's harder than any sword lesson, especially for people like me and you."

"What do you mean?"

"We're not like the others are we? Alonso picked us both up. We don't have what they call *breeding*."

Matthias finished adjusting his shirt cuffs and flattened his hair one last time in the looking glass next to his bed. "How hard can it be? It's just learning how to be polite."

"Yes," said Harry, "just how to be polite." He walked out the door to go to his lesson but not before calling out, "And of course how to *dance*!"

Harry's laughter faded as he skipped down the corridor. Matthias looked at his wide eyes in the mirror and swallowed hard. Dancing? Surely Harry must be joking. For the first time since he'd arrived at the castle he felt genuine fear. Dancing was for girls. Give him half an hour in front of O'Grady with one arm tied behind his back, but not dancing!

The chapel bells rang out two o'clock; he was going to have to hot foot it to the west wing of the castle where Lady Taylor resided. The journey took him ten minutes and as he walked into the drawing room he saw her waiting for him. She was seated at a small table by the window and was pouring tea from a delicate china pot.

The footman who had shown him in gently closed the door behind him but Matthias remained where he was, unsure if he should move without direction. Looking around he took in the room's magnificence. Tapestries and paintings hung from the walls, but unlike other areas of the castle where pictures of dukes and earls adorned the stone, here were works of art. Mythical lands and creatures, men and women depicted in perfect beauty amongst colossal mountains and seascapes. On a gilded table at one end were several sculptures of people Matthias did not recognise and next to that stood an enormous ornate vase, almost as big as he was. The patterns were exotic and mesmerising and Matthias's senses struggled to take in all the beauty that was within this one room.

Then, finally, his eyes fell on Lady Taylor. Her back was to him but Matthias could see she was dressed in white silk. Her golden blonde curls were set up high atop her head and underneath a pale slender white neck was decorated with fine pearls. He stood there for several moments before finally summoning up the courage to make a polite coughing noise.

She turned around, her deep brown eyes met his and he instantly froze. She was beautiful. His gaze fell to floor instinctively and for a moment he felt unworthy even to be in her presence.

"Matthias, I presume?" She spoke with a perfect, soft, sweet voice.

"Yes ma'am," he said, and attempted a bow.

"*My lady*," she corrected. "Please refer to me as *my lady*."

There was no malice in her words; she was just correcting him and her soft smile re-assured Matthias she had taken no offence.

"Sorry, my lady," responded Matthias, and attempted another bow which went slightly less well than the first.

"Will you join me for tea?" she said, and gestured to the empty seat on the other side of the table.

"Thank you, my lady," said Matthias. As he sat down opposite her his eyes caught the shape of her womanly body and her perfume swept over him – it was a smell of sweet fruits, fresh forests and spring blossoms all rolled into one.

She proceeded to serve tea in a meticulous and precise fashion. First a silver jug poured milk into the cup. Then, the pot delivered a wonderfully smelling golden red tea which tanned as it hit the milk. Finally after the offer of sugar, which Matthias duly accepted, he picked up the cup.

Her short intake of breath was directed at Matthias's hands. He felt sure he was doing something wrong; but what? He looked down at his hand holding the impossibly thin china cup before looking back at Lady Taylor. Her fingers caressed the handle of her own cup and the smallest pointed directly into the air away from it.

Matthias had seen Mr Hardy drink in the same fashion. He adjusted his grip, spilt some tea, but finally managed to point his little finger into the air in triumph!

He brought the cup to his lips and drank, or rather, slurped. The lady raised her eyebrows and this time she placed her own cup back on the saucer in front of her.

"Am I to understand you have never taken tea before?"

"I've drank tea?" said Matthias.

Lady Taylor tilted her head to one side in sadness and held her hands together. "My dear boy," she said, "I mean *taken* tea. At a formal occasion such as this; in a parlour, with china and a lady or a gentleman."

"Oh I see," he replied. "No, I haven't. Am I doing something wrong?"

She tutted quietly under her breath and looked awkwardly at him. "Posture, for one. Not only the way you are sitting but the way you are holding the cup and of course your feet."

"Too far apart?"

"Too close together," she replied, tapping the table with each syllable. "All this can be worked on; all of these things can be taught. But that noise dear boy, that frightful noise. That must be *undone*."

He blushed and looked at his feet. They were tight together and he was sitting rather awkwardly but to be fair this was more out of genuine nervousness than any bad habits. True, if he was relaxing in his room with Harry he may well have had his shoes off and his feet firmly under the table, or on it.

"Cake?" said Lady Taylor. He looked down at the impossibly small piece of sponge cake offered to him on a plate alongside a tiny silver fork with only two prongs. What must he do with this? Which hand should he accept it with? Was that even a fork?

He smiled and politely refused. Lady Taylor raised an eyebrow in what he could only assume to be disapproval but said nothing.

"Tell me, Matthias, something of your background."

He happily recounted his days at the abbey explaining the less formal upbringing he had had compared to that of his classmates. He told her of his simple life of Bible lessons, work on the land and play in the orchards. Then, the day Alonso arrived; as was usual when people asked him about his past he left out the events surrounding the fate of Rebecca and the others at the abbey.

Lady Taylor revealed little of herself throughout the exchange, but Matthias did gather that although she spoke perfect English she was originally from France. She had come to England to assist the duke in tutoring his young students in etiquette and also *wooing*. He blushed slightly when Lady Taylor explained what this last part meant.

"Matthias, you may be called upon to charm young ladies or even spinsters in your work. Knowing not only how to speak to a woman, but how to truly understand her, may be as important a weapon as any gun or dagger concealed about your person."

He instinctively looked at the blade sitting on his belt. "If this bothers you my lady I'll take it off," he said, getting to his feet and starting to unfasten his buckle.

"No, no. Not at all," said Lady Taylor. "I am quite used to the sight of arms and, sadly, far worse."

He seated himself again. Looking down at the dagger he realised now that he wore it almost everywhere without even thinking. Maybe this was part of the 'moulding' Father James had told him about. Everywhere, all about the castle, it was not unusual to see children armed with knives, rapiers or even pistols.

Lady Taylor must have read his thoughts because when she spoke her voice was gentle. "This is all so very new to you isn't it?"

He nodded. "Do not worry," she said, "you are in very capable hands here. I have a good feeling about you."

"Thank you, my lady."

She smiled at him and he felt his insides warm. "Matthias. Such an unusual name. Tell me, are you of the house Cortés?"

His eyes scanned around the room, "Erm…"

"Of course," she said, "how silly of me. Mr Hardy insists on no surnames until you've earned them. Such chivalry. I believe when the academy was set up there was a good deal of in-fighting."

"It seems strange," said Matthias. "I only found out my family name recently."

"How odd for you."

"Are you a part of one of the houses?"

She spun her back to him and started to adjust the pins in her hair. "I was once." For a few moments Matthias wasn't sure whether the conversation was over, but she eventually turned back and smiled.

He beamed back, picked up his teacup and drained the remaining contents with a mighty gulp. Lady Taylor raised one eyebrow and forced a smile.

"It would seem we have a lot of work to do. I shall contact Mr Hardy to arrange our next session. For now, I would like to thank you for a delightful tea, Matthias. It has been a pleasure making your acquaintance." She held out a silken gloved hand, her fingers dangling loosely from her wrist.

A cold sweat appeared on Matthias's head. Did he kiss it? Shake her hand? Was she asking for assistance out of her chair? His eyes darted from the hand to her eyes and then back to the extended hand.

"It is traditional to kiss a lady firmly on her hand," she said, softly.

Matthias did so, apologising as his lips bumbled into her knuckles. He stood up smartly, almost to attention, bowed and made his way to the door. As he arrived he turned around, bowed one last time and said, "My lady," then left without looking back.

Chapter 11

The following morning Matthias decided to get up early so he could take a look at the turnout for the tournament. He noticed Harry's bed was already vacant as he made his way to the mustering hall to help himself to some porridge. The hall too was empty. Even though lessons normally didn't begin for another hour it looked like all the other children had similar ideas. Everybody, it seemed, wanted to see what was going on.

He made his way outside and even before he emerged he could hear the cheers. Out in the courtyard a space had been transformed into an arena with the students gathered on all sides. At the far edge Mr Cook was standing in a leather coat, whilst in front of him two boys were fencing with tipped foils. Matthias recognised them; Gerard, whose knife he had snatched on his first day and Alexander.

He spotted Sophie and Harry standing near the action and made his way to them. Just as he arrived a large cheer went up as Gerard, landed a blow. The tipped foil bent up but the impact still sent Alexander stumbling back.

Mr Cook held up his arms, "End of contest." More cheers followed and as Matthias got Harry's attention another boy entered the ring and started to stretch.

"You've missed all the action!"

"I didn't realise it started so early."

"Mr Cook doesn't beat about the bush," said Sophie. "These idiots are going at each other like animals. I think Edgar has possibly lost an eye." She stifled a yawn.

Alexander trudged past them rubbing his ribs. He stopped near the edge of the ring, turned back to look at Gerard who was practising his thrusts before swiping at the floor with his own foil in anger.

He caught Matthias's eyes as he went past, his face looking like thunder and his fists clenched.

"Unlucky," said Matthias.

The blue eyes looked back blankly. "I'm a little out of practice."

"Too much time in the chapel, perhaps?"

Alexander smiled, and a lock of blond hair fell over his eyes which he brushed back. "How are your classes?"

"I'm starting to enjoy it."

"That's too bad," said Alexander, before striding off.

Matthias watched as he walked away, kicking at the dirt before turning to Harry. "Have you been up yet?" he said, trying to sound encouraging.

Harry turned around with a sour look on his face and pointed to a neat fresh cut on the top of his forehead "Gerard took me out in the first bout."

Sophie scoffed, "You were lucky he didn't take your head off!"

"I slipped!" said Harry. "Have you seen this surface? It's dusty and dry. I was wearing the wrong shoes!"

There was a loud roar as Gerard despatched another; this time a girl lay on her side holding her ribs. Even though their padding stopped any serious injury the children were clearly feeling the blows.

Matthias noticed Mr Cook was working his way down through a list and was stood next to O'Grady. It appeared as if the flame haired solider was studying the names in detail and asking O'Grady questions about the combatants.

Back in the arena Gerard strutted around the ring like a cockerel on a farmyard. His chest swelled and he lifted back his head to acknowledge the cheers. Matthias remembered the sneering comments the boy had made when they first met and felt his fist clench.

"You've got to hand it to him," said Harry, "he's taking no prisoners."

"I could teach him a lesson," said Matthias.

"Don't be silly," said Sophie. "He's about a foot taller and has the strength of five men!"

He picked up Harry's leather jerkin off the floor. "What are you doing?" said Harry.

"Skipping a school year!" said Matthias, and he started to make his way around the ring. This was his chance. To show what he was capable of and start to get the real training he deserved. As he approached Mr Cook looked up from his paper with a smile.

"Matthias? What can I do for you?"

"I'd like to put myself forward, sir," he said, with just a hint of shakiness in his voice.

"The contest is only for apprentices or journeymen. I believe you are still a junior?"

"That doesn't bother me. Unless Gerard has any objections?" He looked over at the older boy who merely shrugged.

"Very well then," said Mr Cook. "Matthias please choose your weapon."

Mathias picked up one of the tipped training sabres from a pile on the floor. In all his lessons so far the slashing strokes of the sabre where his strongest attack. A foil or rapier required balance and height. Being shorter, Matthias realised this would be too much of an advantage for Gerard. He practiced a few swift strokes and the blade whistled through the air around him. Finally he walked to the centre of the arena where Gerard was waiting.

As they stood apart only now did a slither of fear trickle into him. Gerard was a good foot taller than him, stronger and with a longer reach. Matthias realised he was going to have to use his speed and agility to outfox the boy. *Attack from the sides and underneath but don't try and take him head on.*

Mr Cook called for silence and then shouted, "Take positions."

The two boys stood to attention and saluted each other with their blades before adopting their relative stances. Gerard with one foot placed behind him stood sideways; the foil resting at an angle from his front thigh, his back arm slightly outstretched with fingers pointing to the rising sun.

Matthias stood facing front; his feet a shoulder width apart and crouching slightly. The blade was pointed high and directly in front of his face; a stance he had been taught by O'Grady. From this position he could bring the blade up or down with equal speed and then direct it at his opponent with a slashing motion from either above or the flanks. All he had to do was make contact with Gerard's torso to score a point and win the bout.

"I'm going to enjoy this," said Gerard, with a sneer.

"En garde!" shouted Mr Cook, and his voice was followed by a roar from the gathered students.

Gerard attacked first. The lunge was straight and true but predictable and Matthias was already prepared to glance the boy's blade sideways with his own. This gave him the opportunity to strike but he suspected Gerard was feigning imbalance and held back.

Sure enough another lunge followed immediately and Matthias stepped sideways as it probed near his stomach. Now was his chance and he brought the sabre down and across Gerard who was momentarily off balance. The blade caught his foil with a clang sending the boy a couple of steps back.

"Still having fun?" said Matthias.

Gerard sneered back and took his stance once more. This time there was a feint and a thrust. The boy's height helped him as Matthias was too far back to retaliate and it was all he could do to parry. The sheer force of steel upon steel sent him staggering backwards as Gerard's infamous strength hit him like an ox.

Breathing, he left himself open for only a second but Gerard had spotted it and lunged again. Matthias dived to his side and rolled onto the floor. When he looked up, thankfully, Gerard was still recovering from his lunge and pulling his foil out of the dirt. Matthias could see from the fire in his eyes that the 'first point' scored might mean more than a scratch.

As he got on to one knee Gerard lunged again. He heard the boys breath grunt out of his mouth and the foil passed within an inch of his ear. He knocked it aside and returned a blow to the boy's legs. His strike was quick, cool and true. Matthias saw his black leggings split open to reveal the creamy skin below, shortly followed by a widening red line were his blade had nicked him. The contest was over...or so he thought.

"First blood! End of the contest!" bellowed Mr Cook, amidst the sounds of cheers. Matthias looked up and saw Mr Cook regard him with a wry smile from the other side of the arena. His two friends stood nearby and he noted with satisfaction that even Sophie was grinning. Harry looked as if he was going to positively explode!

Sophie's warm grin suddenly froze and he saw her eyes dart behind him. Perhaps it was the movement of air or a sense of something but he immediately dived to his right and rolled on the ground again. It was Gerard! He had tried to strike after the contest. The boy's face was red and his eyes blank and lost.

"En garde!" he screamed, and then lunged.

The power completely took Matthias by surprise and he was sent hurtling backwards onto the ground. He felt a sharp pain in his ribs and as his hand touched the area he felt the wetness of his blood. He didn't have time to collect his thoughts as he saw the foil come down at him from above, the flat point catching the sun's rays. Gerard screamed as again Matthias rolled away.

He could see Mr Cook and Mr Hardy running over but it was too late. As he tried to bring his sabre up he felt Gerard's foot crash into his hand. Screaming in pain he had no choice but to release the sword and when he looked up Gerard loomed over him. One foot was crushing his wrist as he held his foil tight, point first, against Matthias's throat.

"Yield!" he shouted.

The blade dug into Matthias's windpipe. "I yield," he croaked.

Footsteps soon followed and he heard Mr Hardy bellow, "Stand down!"

Matthias looked into Gerard's hateful eyes. Was he going to stand down? He thought he saw him grin and his shoulders tense as if preparing to make a final thrust.

But he didn't get the chance. There was a whipping sound of a sword and suddenly the foil was no more at his throat. Both Matthias and Gerard turned to see Mr Hardy wielding his own sword, Gerard's bouncing away to his right. The master took a step toward Gerard and hit him a mighty blow with the back of his hand across the boy's face. Gerard flew to the floor and crumpled near Mathias's feet.

He had never seen the normally calm master so outraged. Mr Hardy breathed heavily and looked around at the gathered crowd. "I believe you all have lessons to go to?" he shouted, with such authority that Matthias struggled to get up himself.

"You stay, Matthias," he said, "and you Gerard." The murmuring and chatter of the children soon quietened as they dispersed to whatever class they were supposed to be at. O'Grady followed them in but Mr Cook stayed behind and walked over to stand next to Mr Hardy. The two boys got to their feet and dusted themselves off.

Matthias tried to stop the flow of blood from the wound to his ribs with little success. He looked across at Gerard who stood in silence, rubbing his face.

"What is the meaning of this?" Mr Cook said to Gerard.

"H-he had no r-right to be in the contest," said Gerard, still surging with fury. "He's not an apprentice!"

"I decided he could enter," cut in Mr Cook. "I made the rules."

Gerard looked at Mr Cook with a sneer. "Well one Cortés aiding another is hardly surprising."

Instantly Mr Cook's face turned white. He regarded Gerard with something approaching disgust.

Mr Hardy sheathed his sword. "How dare you use a family name!"

Gerard gathered himself up to his full height and eyed Mr Hardy with disdain. "Everybody knows. They say he's the image of his father, the traitor."

Matthias tensed his body and had to hold himself back from attacking the boy there and then, a feat made somewhat easier by the sharp look Mr Cook cast him.

Mr Hardy spoke again, but in a more controlled manner, "The house of Pizarro has long held animosity to the house of Cortés, but why you Gerard?"

Gerard looked harshly at Matthias, "He dishonoured me, sir."

"You dishonoured yourself," said Mr Hardy. "Report to my office at four o'clock today for your punishment. Dismissed."

The boy looked at each of the men in turn and finally at Matthias before walking away. As he disappeared into the building Mr Hardy spoke. "You have proven yourself today, Matthias. I will be making the necessary arrangements to have your classes progressed so that you may join your friends as I know you wish to. You are now an Apprentice."

Matthias smiled, it was what he had hoped for. Now he would be able to take part in classes with Harry and Sophie. He thought about teaching Harry a thing or two and couldn't wait to get back and tell him.

"Thank you, sir," he said and made to leave. As he did so Mr Cook had something to say.

"Matthias." He halted and Mr Cook looked at him with a serious face. "Today you came away with an enhanced reputation, honour but more importantly your life. Remember that."

He nodded and hurried back into the castle as the morning sun made its way to the middle of a cloudless sky.

Chapter 12

The entrance to the cave was over a hundred feet high. An enormous gash in the side of the mountain; its sharp edges and detritus littered entrance made it look as if some giant creature had clawed away at the rocks. There was no breeze here even at this height thousands of feet above the sea. Alonso looked around him, always wary when approaching the secret lair of his kin. There were no guards at the entrance. No flaming torches or gate. Few could get here; fewer still would even notice the cave mouth and none had ever entered.

He could see the planes of Spain from these peaks, the purple twilight just brushing the hills and towns. It had been so long that his heart fluttered for a moment with memories. Breathing in deeply, he turned and headed towards the cavern. As he approached the light was slowly swallowed by the mountain; darkness rising around him until finally, some twenty yards inside, the entrance itself was a mere suggestion. That is, to a normal man, but Alonso being a mystic saw things differently. His eyes picked up on the light that others never saw. A purplish tinge to the rocks and rubble on the floor was accompanied by strange colours that could not even be described as he ploughed on ahead through the cave. Far at the back he could see a smaller entrance which led to the meeting chamber.

The three other mystics stood in a circle around a small fire; its smoke climbing so high above them it was lost in the black canopies of rock. They lived solitary lives in the mountains, hardly ever coming across each other and only meeting for trade or, as in this case, an assembly. As Alonso entered one looked up from underneath a hooded cowl.

"Why have you summoned us?"

"I seek advice," responded Alonso, his head bowed at the fire. "My vision has become clouded. I no longer see myself in the boy's future; indeed, I see a strange battle. A curious clash between two men, one of whom may already be dead. Hopefully, my peers will grant me their eyes and we may search together."

"It has been a long time since we all looked for something. What you ask is no small matter."

"No it is not. But it is my duty to try to find out, for in his future I saw my own and perhaps all of ours. I would ask this of you only in the name of my quest."

One of the others looked up now also; tiny slithers of light sparkling from underneath the hood suggested eyes. "Alonso you have been searching for this boy now for too long. Is it not time, perhaps, to admit you were mistaken?"

Alonso shook his head. "No it is not. I found him some months ago and have been in England watching him."

"The last head jerked up, "We received no message?"

"Forgive me brothers, but it was not possible to get one to you. I have been tracking a man on behalf of my employer."

The three mystics appeared to confer, but from across the crackling fire their words were barely audible to Alonso. He had taken a risk coming here, of that much he was certain. Whether his brothers shared his faith in his quest was not his concern. He only knew what his visions had told him.

Mystics saw visions all the time; images and patterns amongst every day signs. Often they would guide people. Kings paid princely sums for their counsel whilst noblemen begged for their advice. Sometimes they gave it, for a price, other times they refused to depart such knowledge. However, one thing had always been constant - the visions were never about themselves. They never saw their own fate or that of their brothers. Mystic's lives were a zigzagging stream of events darting along the surface of time.

But strangely Alonso had seen himself and also a boy. Graver still, he had seen his brothers. He had shared this knowledge with them and asked for their help in his search to find the boy. After it was refused, he had left the caves. That had been ten years ago.

Since then his quest had become entwined with that of the Guard. But that was another story. Right now, he needed help to understand his dreams and only the four of them working together and sharing their minds could do this. The question was, would they help?

Chapter 13

Matthias, Harry and Sophie sat in Mr Butler's secluded classroom, deep inside the castle. It was a cold Sunday outside and the frost had charged down at the castle from the distant mountains. Chilling winds had whipped against the walls and the turrets sending fierce rain and debris at anyone who dared venture out. Most of the other children were in their dormitories, but the three friends had ventured off in search of some solitude.

"Well, I can't understand how that thug Gerard got off so lightly."

"He's shrewd and well connected," said Matthias.

"The boy is, at best, a simpleton." Sophie was sitting on a bench casually browsing through one of the many textbooks that adorned the shelves. Harry was at the back poking a jar that contained some lungs in alcohol solution.

"It was a fair fight," he said, "Gerard knew he'd lost."

Matthias was in Mr Butler's seat with his feet on the table. His hand absent-mindedly touched the point on his ribs where Gerard had wounded him. It had taken several days to begin to heal and the castle physician had changed the bandages again only this morning.

"I've a score to settle with Gerard," said Matthias, "but the important thing is I've been pushed up to the best classes. Looking forward to Monday, Harry?"

Harry turned around from the jars he was looking at, nearly knocking one over. "I'm not scared; if that's what you mean?"

Matthias was due to have his first senior combat lesson tomorrow with O'Grady and the rest of his apprentices – which included Harry. He had been teasing his friend all week about their first practice which, frankly, couldn't come too soon for Sophie. In her opinion the boys' egos were now starting to fill rooms.

Matthias chuckled. "I never said you were Harry! I just said it was going to be fun. What do you think Sophie?"

She looked up from her book, her long black hair dangling over her face. "I wouldn't get over confident if I were you Matthias. Harry is no novice."

"Neither was Gerard," said Matthias.

Sophie returned to her book and smirked.

"What?"

She looked up, "You're forgetting that Harry has certain skills." Her eyes looked to Matthias's right and she nodded in that direction.

Matthias made to look and then too late realised he had been tricked. Harry, unseen and unheard, had snuck up behind him and placed a dagger casually across his throat.

"I don't believe Gerard can do this," he whispered. Sophie chuckled somewhere in the background. Matthias was aware of, but couldn't see, Harry poised somewhere behind him.

He had to concede and Harry gave him a friendly pat on the shoulder and sat down on the chair next to him.

"How do you do that? You literally vanish."

"It's my gift."

Suddenly, outside of the room, they heard footsteps and voices. They all stood up just as the door opened and in walked Mr Hardy, Mr Cook and Alonso.

Their conversation trailed off and Mr Hardy spoke with authority, "What are you doing in here?"

Matthias looked to Sophie and said, "We were just reading our books, sir." As soon as he spoke he realised his own book was lying on the desk unopened and his eyes rolled. Classrooms were technically out of bounds on Sundays but the rule wasn't often enforced.

Mr Hardy's eyes narrowed and he gave his moustache a slight twirl. "Kindly vacate the room please," he said, "both of you."

Matthias nodded and joined Sophie as she made her way to the door and he was almost out of the room when it hit him. *Both of you?* Where was Harry? Sophie's eyes caught his and he knew instantly she was thinking the same thing. What was the idiot up to now? He could get in real trouble. As they left Alonso shut the door firmly behind them.

"What's he playing at?" whispered Sophie.

"I don't know," said Matthias, shaking his head. "You know what he's like."

Sophie stood near the door. "That boy's thirst for excitement is going to get him into real trouble one of these days. Can you hear anything?"

"No," whispered Matthias, "They're speaking quietly. What should we do? We can't wait out here."

"We'd best head back to the mustering hall and wait for him. If he gets caught it's his own fault."

They headed down the gloomy corridor until they arrived at the brightly lit hall where several of the other children where relaxing and playing games. Matthias and Sophie found a secluded corner to sit themselves down in and got their books out under the pretence of study.

They didn't have much of a chance to even begin to feign interest in the texts before a bell started to ring out from the watchtower. Everybody looked up from what they were doing with puzzled expressions.

"It's the alarm," said Sophie. "We need to get outside." Sophie started packing her book in her bag and turned to him. "This doesn't look good. Do you think they caught him?"

"Well if he's in trouble at least we're not involved."

"What do you mean?" whispered Sophie. "We knew he was in the room. If they've found him they'll have our guts for garters as well!"

Matthias looked at Sophie as she ran her fingers through her hair. He knew it meant so much to her to be here that the thought of jeopardising it filled her very bones with dread.

"Don't worry," he said. "We can say we didn't know. Harry's used to getting in trouble." He patted her on the back and then the two friends followed the throng outside.

As they reached the courtyard the wind hit them in their faces but luckily the rain had stopped and the children lined up in their class groups. As they sought their own Matthias and Sophie were stunned to see Harry stood amongst some of their classmates with a big grin.

When they arrived they stood in line behind him and tried not to act surprised. "What happened?" said Matthias.

"I'll tell you later," said Harry. Before they could discuss things any further a silence descended upon the crowd as Mr Hardy made his way to the front and started to address them.

"Until further notice the castle is to be locked down. We have a security concern and so for your own safety nobody is to leave these walls."

A collective groan enveloped the courtyard and the children started to chatter amongst themselves. Mr Hardy made a loud coughing noise – he was not used to having to do so and he looked cross.

"You will be advised when restrictions are to be lifted but until then *nobody* leaves and everybody is confined to their respective wings after lessons. You are all dismissed."

The students started to disperse and make their way back to their various halls and dorms. But Matthias and Sophie grabbed Harry and cornered him underneath a large stained glass window.

"What happened?" said an exasperated Sophie. Harry looked at the pair and waited a suitably long time to build up the tensions, a big soppy grin across his face.

"I found out a secret. You're going to love it!"

"What?" said Matthias.

"We'd better go inside I think," said Harry, nodding towards Mr Butler who was ushering children back into the castle. "Sophie, head to our room and we can talk there."

They mixed in with the swarm of students trickling back to various parts of the castle. However, where Sophie should have turned right for her dormitory she instead turned left for the mustering hall and followed Matthias and Harry straight through to their room just off the back.

Harry strode in and sat back on his bed his hands behind his head. He was clearly relishing being the custodian of whatever secrets he had learned.

"Well?" said Sophie, as she and Matthias pulled up chairs.

"Alright," said Harry, as he settled himself. "So, after you two left I slipped into the shadows behind the large book case. They all sat down on desks and chairs and Mr Cook stood at the front. Apparently Hardy's office was being used by someone for a meeting. Then they start talking about a prisoner."

Sophie and Matthias exchanged excited glances and then stared back at Harry. "Turns out Alonso had been tracking someone and he's finally got his man."

Matthias felt a cold sweat cross his chest. "A prisoner?"

"Yes," replied Harry. "Apparently he's in the cells right now under Mr Cook's guards."

Sophie looked at Matthias with a raised eyebrow. But he wasn't looking at Harry anymore.

"What is it Matthias?" said Sophie.

Matthias stared at the floor. "Did you get the name of the person Alonso brought in?"

"What?"

"The name," he said, "did you hear them mention the name of the prisoner?"

Harry looked to Sophie in confusion and then turned back to Matthias. "Yes. I think they said he was called Balthazar."

Matthias stared into space. Softly, he said the name again, "*Balthazar*." His eyes closed over and both

Sophie and now Harry looked at him with genuine concern.

"Are you alright?" said Harry.

"I'm fine," said Matthias, suddenly straightening himself. He looked at them both and smiled. But the smile was not true. It was a sad smile and it didn't hide the pain underneath it.

Sophie placed her hand on Matthias's. Her deep brown eyes looked at him and for a second he thought he might break down and cry.

"Tell us Matthias," she said. "Tell us who this man is." And with that, Matthias told his story and he did not leave out one bloody detail.

Chapter 14

The three friends sat in silence for some time after Matthias had finished recounting his tale. Harry looked at the floor uncertain of what to say and Sophie merely held onto his hand staring into some faraway distant space. Finally, after several minutes it was the young girl who spoke.

"You must take this opportunity, Matthias," she said, calmly. "I can help you."

Harry's head snapped up. Matthias took a moment to turn Sophie's words over in his mind.

"Wait a minute," said Harry. "You don't really mean that do you?"

"Why not?" said Sophie.

Harry got to his feet in front of the pair. "You mean to waltz into the cells and murder this man? He's guarded by four of Cook's men, or had you forgotten?"

"He's going to be killed anyway, surely?" said Matthias. Sophie nodded.

"Yes, but after a trial. Besides, Matthias, you don't even know if he did it. You never saw his face." Harry looked concerned and turned to Sophie; maybe this was one adventure too big for him.

"I'll know when I look in his eyes."

Harry hadn't finished. "You're not ready for this, Matthias. Let it go." His eyes, that were normally so full of mischief, were pleading with him.

He regarded Sophie, before looking back to Harry, "We'll need you," he said. You can get in there, find out where he is. Maybe even steal a key."

Harry shook his head. "It's too difficult. These men are experts. There's no way I could get into a prison block, let alone back out again, without being discovered."

"Maybe not," said Sophie, "but if you could just get me into the kitchens. I could take care of the rest."

The two boys turned to look at her, their eyebrows raised. "Poison him?" said Matthias.

"We wouldn't need to get anywhere near his cell."

"How could we be sure?" said Harry. "I mean, they might have several prisoners down there. How would we know which meal was his?"

Sophie sighed and started to play with her hair, something Matthias noticed she always did when she was trying to remain calm. "You could watch. Do it a few times and you'll soon see their routine."

"But surely Matthias would want to do it?" he said. "After all, this man murdered *his* sister."

They both looked at him and waited for an answer. Matthias started to think about the man in the abbey. To think about the face he had almost seen. That voice, the harsh whisper. Then, his thoughts turned to his friends. He saw the blood pooling on the floor and children's bodies lying all around him. He imagined the pain they had gone through, their cries for help and their screams. Finally he saw Rebecca's face as she fell, her eyes rolling into the darkness.

Just for a moment he was back there. Back in that room amongst the flames. He looked down and saw a knife in his hand. Startled, he blinked and sat upright.

Sophie and Harry were watching him. Matthias spoke softly. "He's right. I want to do it." The light was failing now and he was covered in shadow.

"I will not rest until I have taken his life and spilt every drop of his blood."

They could barely see his face and they weren't sure if he was looking at them. Sophie started to speak but Matthias interrupted. "I want to look into his eyes as I kill him. I want him to know who I am. I will make this man's last moment one of fear, pain and despair."

He waited to see if either of them said anything. "I need to know if I can count on you, Harry."

"Matthias, I'm your friend. But this…"

"*This* is the big adventure you've always wanted. Everything we've learned; now we can put it in to practice. Otherwise what's the point?"

Harry sighed, his chest sank a little and he sat down again. "I'm with you, Matthias."

He waited to see if either spoke again. Neither did. Finally, Sophie started to discuss their options. She was the calmest and most clinical. Her ideas flowed freely and she even started to draw some simple diagrams. The three sat up late into the night hatching their plan. They all agreed poison was not a possibility if Matthias wanted the kill himself and the only person who could get close enough to even try would be Harry.

He decided he wanted Harry and Sophie to get him inside the cells. After all, he reasoned, they were designed to keep people from getting out, not in. They talked for many hours and subjected each plan to close scrutiny. Eventually Sophie tired and they agreed to sleep on it. She bid the boys farewell and left for her dormitory. Harry said he too was tired and blew out the candle before curling up on his bed.

Matthias remained upright in his seat. The moon was the only source of light now and it spilt into the room from a starless sky coating everything with a pale blue. "I can't sleep," he whispered to Harry, who was already snoring. "I think I'll go for a walk."

He got out of his chair, pulled on his coat and slipped away. Shadows danced across the mustering hall as he made his way toward the chapel. Somehow, even though he was not a pious boy, he felt he might find some peace there.

Making his way through the murky corridors he encountered not a soul. The castle was so quiet, deep inside he couldn't even hear the wind. As he came to the chapel and walked through the doors he looked up. Here, the moon streamed through the stained glass and the colours spread out before him like flowerbeds. It was beautiful. In front of him was Jesus on the cross, the disciples and several saints all in prayer. The images that he had seen a hundredfold in daylight looked different. It was something about the moonlight. Its colour, its coldness and its clarity.

As he sat down on a pew he thought perhaps this clarity could somehow give him the answer he needed. He toyed with the dagger and long into the night he sat in front of the altar, but not at prayer.

To murder even an evil man, was beyond forgiveness in the eyes of the Lord. His uncle had told him this much only yesterday in another one of his talks. The old man had even offered Matthias a place at his side, here in the chapel after his training, but he had refused.

He looked to the monk's door and could just make out the faint flickering yellow light of a candle. Surely his uncle wasn't awake at this hour? He eased himself up and softly walked over to the corridor that took him down to the small gloomy study. The old man was nowhere to be seen but he had left a candle burning on the table. Matthias sat down and started to glance through some of the books. It looked like his uncle had been reading through the works of his predecessor Father Morant again.

What had he called him? A historian, of sorts. He'd disappeared in mysterious circumstances, Matthias was sure of that. He picked up one of the books, "*A Short History of Miguel López de Legazpi.*" On the front cover was a crest with black and yellow stripes; much like a honey bee.

He continued browsing and found more books; each one a history of someone. There were many names – Pizarro, de Ojeda and Nunez! He froze and looked at the book in his hand. "*Vasco Nunez,*" it read. The crest on the cover featured a dragon underneath what looked like a seahorse. He opened the book and on the first page found a family tree. His finger traced downwards until he came to the name he knew would be there – *Balthazar*. He said the word under his breath.

That's when he noticed something that puzzled him. Vasco Nunez was born in 1475. Balthazar, his son, was born in 1550. Matthias blinked and looked again. There were no grandchildren, and all of Vasco's other children were born around the same time.

How could this be? The year was 1817. Impossible. He looked at the rest of the family tree but it stopped there. No more children, no marriages and no deaths. Vasco Nunez and his family were still alive if this book was to be believed, but it was clearly out of date. Balthazar must have had a great grandfather with the same name. Thumbing through the pages he found even more details on Vasco's life; his ascension to titles, battles and triumphs.

He picked up another one: "*A History of the Pizarro Family.*" The crest was faint and worn but Matthias could make out two bears either side of a tree. He opened the pages and looked inside at the diagram showing the lifelines of Francisco Pizarro and his sons and daughters – all eight of them.

Matthias searched until he could find another candle and lit it. Francisco was born in 1476. His children were born around 1500 onwards; so were their children and their children's children. The family tree was enormous and complex, but only a few of the names had dates of death.

Matthias regarded the book. Of course, he thought, Father Morant must not have finished his work. These were ancient histories that were incomplete and missing all the relevant deaths.

"History interests you does it?" said a voice from the shadows.

Matthias turned with his hand already on his dagger. Stood in the doorway was Alonso; his great hulk blocking the old stone exit and his single eye reflecting the candlelight.

"My uncle doesn't mind me being here," said Matthias.

"I have no doubt," said the mystic. "Although I imagine he would prefer you were accompanied at this hour. But you haven't answered my question."

He looked at the books scattered on the table and the names with their fanciful crests and shields stared back at him.

"These books make no sense. The family trees are only half complete."

Alonso stepped forward and walked to the table. He picked up one of the books and Matthias couldn't help noticing it was that of Vasco Nunez.

"Interesting you should use that *exact* phrase," he said softly. "Some might say that these men's lives were only half complete."

"What happened to them?" said Matthias.

"There are many tales associated with the names you see in these books. Each family has its histories and tragedies. Each name brings with it a story. Father

Morant documented these stories, as far as he could. You see, the stories themselves are not yet finished."

"I don't understand."

Alonso opened the book and started to flick through the pages. "One name, one book in particular, I imagine caught your eye. Yes?"

"Yes."

"You seek revenge on this man?"

"Yes."

The mystic appeared to consider this and after some thought he nodded. "It is a difficult thing to take a man's life. Only at the very last second will you know for sure if you can complete the undertaking. A king can send an army to their deaths without blinking an eye; but to kill a man in cold blood…"

Alonso stepped forward, his tall frame blocking the light from the candle. "You need to be up close."

Matthias looked at the floor and imagined himself for a moment holding a knife to the throat of Balthazar Nunez.

"Before you begin this journey though, I would suggest you look for something." Alonso placed the volume he held on the table amongst the others.

"Another book?"

Alonso smiled, "Yes, the one book missing from that pile." Matthias looked down at the names. They seemed to form a pattern in his mind.

"Cortés," said Matthias, softly his lips barely moving. "My family. Where is it?"

"I do not know. But perhaps your uncle does."

He looked down again at the pile. When he looked up Alonso had vanished.

Chapter 15

Father Morant's handwriting was delicate and Matthias could read it well enough. But he didn't understand the meaning.

Michael Cortés - born 1502

"I was going to wait until you were old enough to explain this," said a voice from behind him, instantly recognisable as that of his uncle.

"Until I was old enough?"

The old man sat down on a pew at the end of the bed. Matthias kept looking at the pages in his hand going over each word and number again and again. He'd gone to his uncle's room, to find out what Alonso had meant. The monk had been sleeping, but the book was there on the shelf with others. It had been easy to spot; it was the only one with dust on the shelf in front of it where it had laid undisturbed.

"You are very special. You are a child of *The Fountain*." Matthias turned to stare at the old man. He was smiling, wanting to let Matthias know how much he cared.

"My father, your grandfather, was a conquistador. He and six other men ruled vast areas of what we now know as the Americas. They were adventurers, soldiers and their undertakings brought them much wealth; most of which found its way back to Spain. But one treasure they kept for themselves."

Matthias made his way to the pew and sat next to his uncle. Eyes focused and mouth slightly open he listened as his uncle continued.

"It was Vasco Nunez who first heard the tale. Deep in the jungle he'd come across a tribe of natives who told him of a fountain that granted great powers of life to any that drank from its waters. At first he believed it to be nothing more than a story.

"But the more time he and his party spent with the tribe the more he noticed how they seemed somewhat different. They were all exceptionally fit and healthy, even the elders. Some were able to leap up trees like apes and others run as fast as leopards. Slowly, he came to the conclusion they were a miracle race of what he referred to as 'God's Children.' You see he theorised that whatever had done this to them was a gift from the almighty.

"And so, the young Vasco studied them; indeed some of *his* work is in these books. From their life stories and descriptions he was able to piece together the history of the tribe. He was able to make educated guesses at their ages from what they could tell him about the seasons. Many looked younger than him but he deduced some were several hundred years old."

Matthias straightened, his head popping back on his shoulders.

"When Vasco shared this knowledge with his six fellow conquistadors they organised an expedition to find the fountain, although unknown to them at the time, they all had different views on what they would do when they found it."

"When was all this?" said Matthias.

"It was the year of our Lord 1498. Over three hundred years ago."

Matthias gazed at the old man. Here, in his simple room, illuminated by only moonlight he looked frail and somehow older. His own father was born in 1502; it said so in the book in his hand. James was younger, but by how much?

"May I ask a question?" said Matthias.

Father James laughed and looked down at his robes in embarrassment, "You want to know how old I am don't you?"

The monk's eyes shone with mischief. His hand took Matthias's and he clenched it tight as he spoke.

"This October I will be three hundred and four years old. I too am a child of the fountain Matthias, but different from yourself."

"How?" asked Matthias.

"I will come to that." The old man paused to collect his thoughts before continuing. "So, the men set off into the jungle. Deep and far they travelled until they discovered an ancient and long abandoned city. There, they found the fountain. And they drank from it."

Matthias thought he saw pain cross the old man's face and the monk looked solemn as he continued his story.

"They found themselves rejuvenated. Sickness cured, their strength grew and they became convinced they had a gift from God. Then, they argued.

"The seven men were split on what to do with their discovery. Vasco was the most vocal; he said they must take as much of the water as they could and return to Spain. They would be kings. Raise an army of soldiers; each with the strength of ten men and the speed of cheetahs. They would create a force of such power and fortitude as to be unstoppable. Spain could conquer Europe; defeat the Ottoman Empire; take back the holy lands. A Crusade."

Matthias looked at his uncle, "What happened next?"

"Vasco had supporters; two men Balboa and de Soto agreed. Your grandfather and the others disagreed. They thought it too great a power to bestow upon men and they were right. They suggested the fountain be kept a secret and they all take counsel. A fight broke out. Swords were drawn and one man, Legazpi, fell. Vasco and his two supporters fled. Your grandfather and his two comrades Pizarro and de Ojeda made their way back. Thus began the 'War of the Fountain.'

"Over the years the families grew in power and wealth. Some attributed this to the fountain itself, but in truth the men used their gains from the Americas to buy favour and the longevity of their lives helped them assail to positions of power.

"Every so often they would fake their death and resurface again years later when nobody could recognise them. The treachery continued though. You see, Cortés's have a great history of cartography and your grandfather was the only one in the group making a map. He was and still is the only person who knows where the fountain lies.

"Over the years he has kept it hidden from the world. Some say within a great tomb others say it was buried under a mountain. My father has never told anyone. To this day Vasco and his 'Legion' seek the fountain to unleash its power on the world for God's glory, or so they say."

Matthias found himself leaning back, slightly shaking his head, unable to digest much of what he had been told. He looked out of the window into the courtyard. The first trickles of sunrise were beginning to spill over the battlements and into the castle. Soon the other students would be waking, but he felt as if time had frozen.

"You mentioned I am special," he said finally. "Why?"

Father James looked to the books Matthias had brought with him. "Each of the men bore children who, like them, had certain powers of life and strength. My father had two sons; myself and your father, Michael. Look through these books and you will see generation after generation. As each child was born, married and had children of their own, so the powers were slowly diluted."

Matthias stared, "But–" he started to say.

"You, are the exception. Your father married another child of the fountain. Your mother was Margaret Pizarro. Nobody else was born of such stock." As he said this Father James casually waved his hand at the walls.

"The castle?" said Matthias.

"Precisely. The children here are all, in some way, offspring of the houses of Cortez, Pizarro or de Ojeda although the bloodlines are very diluted by now. Several hundred years have passed and many generations have been born and died. But they are the descendants and each can, usually, trace their bloodline back to one of the families."

"Usually?" said Matthias.

"Some," replied his uncle, "your friend Harry for instance, were born out of wedlock. The daughter of a lady who made a mistake? A young master sowing his seed? We will never know how some of these children got their powers, but Alonso does his best to seek them out and bring them here were they can be trained and schooled."

"And me?"

The old man turned to look at him. "You must understand Michael felt you were too valuable to lose. You are a direct descendant of Hernan Cortez and Francisco Pizzao. The bloodline will be most strong with you."

Strangely, he found his thoughts drifting to his days at the abbey. The long summers which he'd never much counted before. "Can I expect to live so long a life?"

"I think so."

One final piece of all this fell into place.

"Rebecca, the other children at the abbey? Balthazar, was looking for us wasn't he?"

"Yes," he said. "Undoubtedly Vasco has heard of you and sees you as a threat. At least, that is Mr Hardy's theory."

Father James's eyes glistened. "It was not your fault Matthias." He held him at arm's length and looked into his eyes.

"They found Nunez," he said. "They are going to bring him to justice. As a man of faith I cannot condone their actions but I will not pray for his soul after such evil."

They stood together for some time until sunrise turned into morning. Matthias didn't share the fact that he knew Nunez was being kept in the castle. Nor did he share his intentions. In need of some sleep, he bid his uncle farewell and headed back to his room.

On his way back he decided to take the long way around the outskirts of the castle and get some fresh air. The icy morning breeze was sharp and he brought his collar up around his exposed neck.

In the courtyard, something caused him to squint against the low sunbeams and it made him stop in his tracks. Two men were moving a large coach into the stables. They grunted and groaned as they guided it through the giant doors. Matthias picked up his pace and headed back to the mustering hall.

Chapter 16

At breakfast Matthias sought out his friends and found both huddled over their meals in a corner. Sophie was studying a book but somehow noticed Matthias approach and looked up at him with a smile.

Harry raised an eyebrow. "Where did you get to last night?" he said, as Sophie looked on.

Matthias sat down. "I went for a walk. I needed to think." He picked up some bread and poured a cup of milk from a jug. All around them the hall was busy with children taking their breakfast and gossiping away in pockets. Somehow, in their corner, it seemed silent and darker than the rest of the room. Perhaps a portent of the subject they were certain to turn their attentions to, thought Matthias, and indeed it was Harry who first broached it.

"So," he said, looking around to see if anyone was in earshot, "did you come up with a plan?"

Matthias smiled. Sophie put down her book. "Well?"

He turned to Harry. "Do you still have to clean the stables on Sunday mornings?"

Harry frowned. "Of course, you know I do. I've got two more weeks of it!"

Sophie looked across the table and raised her eyebrows in confusion. Harry sighed, "I tried to borrow a pony to go out trekking a couple of weeks ago and the stable master caught me. He said I had to clean the stables for a month or he'd tell Mr Hardy."

Sophie gave a little chuckle. "How did you get caught?" she asked.

"Blasted pony bolted and threw me!"

"That's not all it did," said Matthias.

"Can we stick to the matter in hand, please?" said Harry.

"Of course." But Matthias let Sophie know with a quick wink he'd share the rest of Harry's misfortune with her later.

"I was walking past the stables last night on my way back," he continued, "when I saw a new coach. A big metal coach with an iron door."

"A prison coach?" said Sophie. "They must be taking Nunez on somewhere else."

Harry shrugged, "So what's the plan?" Children were starting to leave for lessons and it was getting empty in the mustering hall.

"I'm not going to break into the prison," said Matthias. "It's too hard. You were right; I'd never get past the guards."

"You're going to hide in the prison coach," said Sophie.

He nodded and pointed at Harry. "But I need *you* to show me how."

Sophie now too turned her gaze to their friend. Harry's eyes narrowed as he digested what had been said. His fingers drummed on the table and he scratched his chin.

"You want to hide in the coach so that when he's put in you're not seen? Then, I'm assuming, when you're safely away from the castle on the open road you'll kill him? Finally, the tough part – you'll need to get out of the prison coach. Did I miss anything?"

"No," said Matthias.

Harry thought for what seemed like minutes before finally answering. "It may be possible. Let's go and take a look at the coach."

The three friends got up from the table and made their way outside towards the castle's stables. The journey took several minutes as not only was the building on the opposite side, but all the corridors were filled with the usual morning mixture of students and teachers hurrying and barging to get to where they were supposed to be.

Eventually, they got to the courtyard and as they rounded the corner all three looked up at the enormous and decorative structure. The stables were almost as ancient as the castle itself which some say was hundreds of years old. However, they were of a different construction and had clearly been added on later. Great white stone soared upwards and pillars surrounded the two giant doors at either end. Crows sat idly on top staring downwards and letting out the occasional squawk as the wind ruffled their feathers.

The door was open and the three headed towards it; trying to blend in with the other children crossing the courtyard. Inside, the palatial roof stretched back above dozens of stalls extended down each side. Each one had a door that split in two across the middle allowing a hatch through which the animals could be looked after.

"Looks like there's a class out on the ponies," said Harry, as the three nosed through the empty compartments.

It was true, there didn't seem to be a soul around. Harry popped his head around one door, looked inside and reappeared quickly. "The tack room is empty so I guess Joe the stable master is gone too."

"Where was the coach?" said Sophie.

Matthias pointed to the other end of the great building where another giant door was sealed shut from within. "I saw them wheel it in that end." The three made their way there, passing more stalls and rooms full of feed and equipment.

As they reached the end they found a large chamber. In it was the carriage and it was Harry who spotted the tracks on the cobbled floor where dirt and wet had been brought in on the wheels of the giant metal box.

The three approached softly. Harry was first to reach the contraption. It stood at least as tall as two men and the limbers stretched forward enough for six horses to pull it. The monstrous wagon was not only strong, but fast.

The door was solid metal with a small grill so the prisoner could be viewed within. It was open and Harry pulled it wide before peering in. Sophie and Matthias stepped closer to take a look. Inside was a single wooden bench attached to the side and nothing else. The metal cell was designed not for comfort, but security. It was square but with a high roof on top of which were seats for the guards and driver.

"There's your spot," said Harry, pointing upwards. Matthias followed his gaze to the dark alcove about five feet above the bench. There a large ledge, presumably for storage and his eyes traced along the wall downwards to an iron ring on the floor; for the prisoners shackles.

"The roof?" said Matthias.

"No," said Harry, "the shelf. Watch." He leapt inside and spreading his arms and legs hoisted himself up to the top. As he reached it he stretched himself out further using the walls for purchase and finally came to rest flat against the ledge. With a foot in each of the front corners and an arm held against one of the other two he was hardly visible to the naked eye as the cell itself was enveloped in darkness.

"I don't know," said Matthias, "I can still see you."

"I'll blacken your face with soot and lend you some of my gear. You'll blend in like a shadow."

Sophie looked impressed. "You wouldn't need to stay there long. As soon as they shut the door and you were on the road you could do it. Then it's just a matter of getting out." She smiled to herself, paused for thought and then slammed the door shut.

The bang made Matthias jump and Harry yelp with surprise. There was a loud clatter which sounded much like Harry hitting the floor of the cell via the bench.

Sophie pressed her ear up against the door and swung down the bolt outside. "Can you get out?" she shouted, through the grill.

Harry's flustered face appeared moments later. "That was unnecessary," he said.

Matthias held back laughter as Harry looked with contempt at Sophie through the bars. He rattled the door and looked carefully at the iron rods before disappearing beneath the hatch. There was a loud crack and then a metallic click and amazingly the door swung open. Harry stepped out onto the footstep putting something that looked like a blunt, flat knife back inside his jacket.

He looked smugly at Sophie and turned to point at the door. "There's a small gap between the door frame and the lock lever at the bottom." Matthias popped his head into the carriage and looked down.

"Underneath the hinges - here." Harry indicated a small hole in the wooden door just beneath the black iron casing.

"If you can push up hard enough it'll unlock the door from within. I've seen this kind before." Harry looked oblivious to the implications of what he had just said but Matthias had to ask.

"You've been in one?" he said.

"Just the once."

He and Sophie waited in anticipation of the story but were cut short by the sound of approaching footsteps echoing towards them.

Two figures cast a shadow on the far wall as daylight stretched down the length of the stables around them. There was no time to hide so the only option was to try and not look guilty. They relaxed slightly when the scowling figure of Gerard and his friend Evan turned the corner.

"What's going on?" he said. The boy's face was a permanent scowl and Matthias had been trying to avoid him since the fight. His friend Evan's weasel-like features were a permanent sneer and his greasy black hair lay flat across his forehead. He was wiry and thin but was known to be quick with a blade.

"I don't think Mr Hardy would like to know you've been sniffing around here," said Evan, in a raspy voice. His bright green eyes looked at Sophie in a way that made Mathias's stomach turn. She looked back at him, her own eyes widening.

Gerard strode forward towards the nearest of the three, Harry, who was perched on the steps of the carriage. "You've no business here. Get out before I report you."

"Report you?" Harry scoffed.

"Yes, *report*. I'm on watch duty for three months."

"Ah, so that was your punishment. It's a shame it wasn't shovelling dung." Harry kicked at some straw on the floor, sending it onto Gerard's boots as he stood up.

Gerard stepped forward, enraged. "If you want to make a fight of this then I'm more than happy." He put one hand on the knife on his belt, to his side, Matthias saw Evan do the same.

"Don't!" warned Matthias, catching Harry's eye. Although angry, he realised there was a greater quarry. All they had to do was leave and they would arise no suspicion. But then, he saw Harry inhale and puff up his chest squaring up to Gerard. Whether through wanting to prove a point or protecting his pride in front of his friends, Harry was about to cause trouble.

"Harry," said Matthias, stepping forward and positioning himself between the two. "Please?" His eyes begged. He turned to face Gerard. "We were just looking."

The thug scoffed and looked down at him. He stepped closer, purposefully head to head; so close that Matthias could smell the sweat coming from his shirt.

"You come here uneducated, untrained and ill-mannered and think to join us? We don't want you."

"Get lost, Gerard," said Harry, from behind. The brute pushed forward into Matthias who somehow managed to block him.

"Harry, go!" he said, turning to his friend. "Meet me back at the dorm."

"What?" said Harry, taking a step back from the affray. "Don't you want to teach him a lesson?"

At this Gerard roared and shoved Matthias aside to get to Harry who promptly darted behind the coach and disappeared.

"Harry," shouted Sophie, "there are more important things than this."

Gerard began circling the coach. He snarled as he checked under the wheels and round the back. Confused he appeared from the other side and looked up only to see Harry sitting on top of the vehicle smiling.

"Harry!" shouted Matthias, and this time the boy stopped smiling and looked down at his friend's face. "Please, let's go!"

Harry nodded glumly and slid down off the black metal roof landing like a cat in front of Gerard. The two boys squared up to each other one final time before Matthias finally dragged his comrade away. Sophie followed too, but Gerard and Evan remained behind watching them leave. Suspicious of what they had been up to the two boys turned their attention to the coach. The three friends hurried back through the stables and burst outside.

"We don't need that kind of attention, Harry!" Sophie gave him an elbow in the ribs to make her point. "Now Gerard is going to be wondering what we were up to!"

"Relax, he doesn't know anything."

The clock struck nine signalling it was time for their lessons. Matthias had another session with Lady Taylor for which he was already late; and lateness wouldn't be tolerated.

Harry stretched and muttered something about making his way to the firing range and Sophie said she would be in the library. The three parted company and arranged to meet that night. The final part of their plan was still missing though. Now they knew where but they didn't know when. How could they find out when would Balthazar Nunez would be leaving the castle?

Chapter 17

Matthias noticed the morning drag with Lady Taylor. Although he usually found the woman such enchanting company, today all he could think about was Nunez.

The elegant lady sat at the table opposite him in her chamber where they were practising a formal meal amidst the rich shower of rugs, tapestries and cushions. The gold silks and white laces of her dress ruffled and whispered as she leaned forward in her seat to eat her meal, pecking at it rather like some delicate bird.

Matthias looked down at the knife and fork before him as if they were some strange objects from a foreign land. He poked the fork at a slice of veal on the plate and brought the knife around in a slow and delicate cutting motion as he had been instructed. Luckily he wasn't hungry as it was slow progress.

They were interrupted by Lady Taylor's servant knocking at the door. He entered with a small silver plate upon which there was a sealed letter. She thanked the man with the softest of smiles and her golden hair rippled like waves as she looked down to read it.

She broke the wax seal and Matthias noted that once finished, she re-read it and this time followed the words on the paper softy with her lips. When she returned back to the meal her eyes were flat and lifeless.

"I am so sorry but you must excuse me. I have to leave immediately. Thank you for your time today."

She stood up and Matthias immediately raised himself from his seat. She turned and gathered her gowns behind her as she left the room. On her way she threw the letter into the fireplace. Or at least she attempted to. In her haste she didn't notice it bounce off the side of a lump of coal and float underneath the grate. Matthias waited until he was sure he was alone before he picked it up to read.

My Lady,

Your brother Balthazar leaves these walls tomorrow at sunrise. Now would be a good time for you to say farewell.

Mr Hardy.

He re-read the letter. His eyes moved to the door where the woman had just vanished and he breathed deeply. Lady Taylor was Balthazar Nunez's sister?

He looked at the signature of Mr Hardy noting the way he curled the last letter of his surname. There was no doubt the handwriting was his; he'd seen the signature on many a report. He threw the letter into the fire and hurried out of the chamber heading straight back to his room. Dashing past a confused Harry, who managed a greeting, he ignored it and opened the trunk at the end of his bed. Underneath various kit and weapons he found the books he had taken from his uncle's study.

There at the top was the Nunez family chronicle. He opened it and turned straight to the family tree which had only ever really contained one name for him. This time he looked along the branch at the man's siblings. There she was. Maria Nunez; born 1547. His older sister!

Next to her name was another; that of her husband, Frederick Taylor. Born 1544 died 1572. They were married in 1568. She was a widow! Matthias sat on the end of his bed with a soft thud as he tried to make sense of the facts.

So there was a Nunez amongst them. Teaching them! How could these people be sworn enemies? He had half-forgotten Harry was even there when his friend asked him what was the matter.

"Go fetch Sophie. She needs to hear this."

Confused, Harry nodded and darted out of the room. Whilst he was gone Matthias contemplated what the reaction would be to him taking this man's life. He was so fond of Lady Taylor, but this felt like a betrayal. How come Mr Hardy hadn't mentioned it? How certain could they be of where her allegiances lay? Maybe she was a spy?

Sophie arrived after being dragged from her chemistry, a flask of some foul liquid still in her hand.

"This had better be important," she said, "I was in the middle of researching something which may help your plan."

The three sat down and Matthias told them of the note but didn't mention the books of Father Morant as he had still not told them who his own father was.

"I can't believe it!" said Harry. "A Nunez here, in the castle? Right under our noses!"

Sophie shook her head. "Mr Hardy is obviously aware of who she is. He must trust her. Perhaps she has no fondness for the Legion's work either?"

"No matter," said Matthias, "this letter tells us he leaves tomorrow. We must act tonight."

"Agreed," said Sophie, and with that she decided to tell them what she had been researching; but when she enlightened them the two boys shrugged.

"Flash powder?" said Matthias, "I've never heard of it."

"Nor should you have. Its exact formula is a very well-kept secret." Sophie reached inside her leather satchel and produced a tattered dusty book. The letters on the front looked like none Matthias or Harry had ever seen before.

"It comes from Arabia," she continued. "Its chemical formula, in essence, is very similar to gunpowder except more volatile. It can be ignited kinetically."

Matthias and Harry stared at each other blankly. Sophie sighed and gave a sideward grimace. "I mean you can explode it just by throwing it. You won't need a pistol or rifle."

Matthias sat up. "I can use it on Nunez?"

"Yes and no," said Sophie, confusing the two boys even further. "Flash powder was the creation of the Hashshashin."

"Who are they?" said Harry.

"They were a secret society of assassins from Arabia who were created around the time of the crusades hundreds of years ago. Some say they are still alive, though they lay silent since the Holy Wars but will one day rise again to destroy the wicked infidels of the west."

"The who?" said Harry.

"I think she means us," said Matthias, nudging him in the ribs.

"Thought I'd check," said Harry. "So what can this powder do?"

"If used in the correct quantities you can make bombs that, although small, can achieve significant effects. Blindness, confusion even loss of hearing."

"Why not make a bigger one?"

"It's too volatile. But get it right and you can leave your foe completely at your mercy and they are easy to conceal about your person."

Matthias sat back and thought for a moment. If Sophie was right this could be just the distraction he would need in order to catch Nunez off guard. He'd thought about pistols or a rifle but getting hold of the equipment, let alone the powder and charge, would have been difficult and could arouse suspicion.

"I'll need to practice," he said.

"Of course," replied Sophie. "I'll have some ready for this evening. Maybe we could sneak into the forest?"

"But we're locked down?" said Mathias.

Harry nodded. "I can help you there. I know a good way out around by the kitchens. Even under lockdown it's easy. The trouble's getting back in. We'll need someone to stay behind and lower a rope."

"I'm happy to do that," said Sophie. She got up and smiled at the two boys, "I don't like loud bangs anyway. I'll meet you by the kitchens at eight."

As Sophie left Harry got up to follow her and grabbed his satchel. "I have to go back to the range. Wilson reckons I've been losing my concentration so he wants me to take some extra practice."

He winked at Matthias, "See you at eight o'clock."

In the cool darkness of the room Mathias lay back on his bed and dozed only to be awoken by the church bells chiming seven. He was so tired he had slept all afternoon; his last few nights had been restless and it was starting to take its toll. Lord alone knew how he was going to get to sleep tonight but he promised himself he would try. He went to the mustering hall to see if he could manage some supper and was relieved to find some bread and cheese still lying around unclaimed.

Taking it, he returned to his chamber to eat whilst he prepared for tonight. His plan was to go straight to the stables after testing the flash powder in the forest and then lay in wait.

He packed his small kitbag with the black clothes Harry had provided, two knives, the rest of the food and his water canteen. Then he made his way to the back of the kitchens. It was still only a quarter to eight but Harry was already there. Smoke billowed out of the chimneys where the evening's fires were dying and the sunset bounced off the castle brickwork giving everything an orange glow.

Harry stood next to the large barrels used to store rotten food. The smell of the decomposing meals wasn't pleasant but they didn't have long to wait before Sophie joined them. She appeared around a corner in the dingy light carrying a small sack cautiously in one hand.

"They're in here," she said. "Be very careful." She opened it and the two boys peered inside. What they could make out where several small parcels of paper moulded in to rough ball shapes.

"What do we do?" said Harry.

Sophie raised an eyebrow and quickly sealed the bag handing it to Matthias. "You need to throw them at something. A hard stone or wall, possibly a tree and then make sure you turn away."

"Have you tried one out yet?" asked Matthias.

"No," said Sophie, "someone would hear."

"So I'm holding in my hand a bag of experimental bombs?"

"That would be correct," replied Sophie, with not a trace of humour.

He exhaled and then turned to Harry. "Let's go. Sophie, we'll need you to lower a rope back down the walls in an hour. Harry will signal with a bird call."

"I'll be here," she said. "Good luck!"

Harry led the way over to the waste area and ducked behind one of the outhouses and Matthias closely followed.

"We need to be careful," whispered Harry. "We're still under lock-down so there are probably some people on watch duty, perhaps even Gerard. We won't know until we get up there though."

"What do you suggest?" said Matthias.

"I'll go first, and let you know if it's clear."

Without further discussion Harry made his way across the yard to an alcove at the foot of the walls. He came back holding a rickety ladder which he held up against the stone face. At this part of the castle the walls were reachable from the ground due to the drop being bigger on the other side. From the top and, with the assistance of a rope, the forty feet or so down was climbable.

The two scaled the ladder onto the stone parapets, Harry first and then Matthias. As they neared the top they were immediately hit by heavy gusts of wind raging their way over the castle's walls. Harry turned to look at Matthias as he ascended the final steps and took a rope out of his knapsack. He tied one end around an iron hook that was sticking out of one of the turrets with some complicated knot Matthias hadn't seen before. He gave it a good tug to check its strength and then hurled the remainder over the walls. He gestured to the rope to Sophie who nodded from below, she would have to climb up and hide it once they were over.

"Alright," he shouted, above the wind. "Watch me closely; feet first and try to guide the rope between your shoulders."

Harry went over the top and began to climb down. The wind was now whipping in their faces and the rope flailed like some un-caged animal. As he neared the bottom he jumped the final few feet and then signalled up for Matthias to begin his descent.

He took the rope with some trepidation and climbed over the side. It burned his hands as he lowered himself slowly but Harry shouted for him to use his legs more on the walls to take some of the strain away. This helped and the pain, in his shoulders at least, ceased. When he reached the bottom Harry was eager to move lest they be spotted.

They reached the woods without event and managed to find a small clearing not too far in to be in total darkness, but far enough that they wouldn't attract attention or be heard.

Matthias reached inside the bag and pulled out one of the paper bombs. He looked at it and raised an eyebrow. Harry shrugged and pointed to a large boulder near a tree which prompted Matthias to throw the device against it.

The resulting bang and flash nearly knocked the two boys off their feet. The light was so bright that both were completely blinded by it. Matthias could see the imprint of the tree and boulder in a multitude of colours on the inside of his eyelids but other than that everything was white. The noise was so loud that neither could hear anything and when they both could finally see they couldn't hear the other speak.

Harry was crouched on one knee holding his hands against his ears and grimacing. Matthias looked over at him from where he had stumbled to the floor. He shouted to ask if he was hurt, but couldn't even hear his own voice. Harry waved back and mouthed something.

Both looked a sorry sight rubbing their eyes and holding their ears dazed and confused amongst the dead leaves. Harry again shouted something that Matthias couldn't hear but in the end resorted to holding his thumb up to show he wasn't injured. Eventually, the buzzing died down and he could just about hear Harry say, "I was waiting for you to give a signal!"

"Sorry," said Matthias, "I forgot we were supposed to turn away."

Harry groaned and got to his feet. He walked over to the boulder by the tree where only a black smudge showed any trace of the explosion. "It doesn't cause any damage," he said wiping the stone, "just the noise and the flash. This could be really useful if you need to escape."

Matthias got up and gave his eyes another tender rub. "How long do you think it lasted – ten, twenty seconds?"

"Long enough," said Harry.

The two boys waited for a few minutes until the effects completely wore off before trying again. Although this time Matthias counted down from three and the two turned away from the flash covering their ears.

"Definitely better," said Matthias, although the thunderous bang was still excruciatingly loud and they again felt the dizziness and confusion associated with an explosion at such close quarters.

"Let's get back," said Harry. "I think it's time we took one last look at the coach."

Harry turned and walked off and Matthias was about to join him when he thought he saw a movement out in the forest far to his right. The light was disappearing quickly as the sun set and the blackness of the trees was gradually spreading outwards. But there it was again; a flash of white, almost like a ladies dress. Darting between two trees, then on to another and another. The figure had, at first, been heading toward them but now Matthias was sure it was moving away.

He turned to shout Harry but his friend was gone. He looked back and now the figure had been joined by two other shapes; where they shadows? Animals? Was the forest playing tricks on him?

He made after Harry; whoever or whatever was out there was of no concern to him. Undoubtedly the noise had attracted someone; but if they were members of the Guard he would already be on his way to Mr Hardy's office by now.

He ran towards the edge of the forest and searched out Harry. "Where did you get to?" said his friend.

"I thought I saw something, someone."

"Probably just a deer," said Harry, still rubbing his ringing ears.

They made their way back to the castle walls where they heaved themselves up the rope Sophie made sure was dangling from the turret. She greeted them behind the kitchens with a wave as she stepped out of the shadows.

"Well?" she said.

"Successful test," said a slightly dishevelled Harry.

Chapter 18

The three decided to try and sleep for a few hours with a view to getting up before dawn to head down to the stables. Sophie suggested it would be best to move about the castle when most people were asleep and the boys agreed.

When Matthias and Harry quietly made their way to the mustering hall, shortly before sunrise, Sophie was already there. She and Harry had agreed to keep a lookout at the stable entrance whilst Matthias hid himself, before giving a signal when the prisoner was on his way.

They reasoned it would be hard for them to move Nunez so some sort of cover story would once again be arranged. They were not disappointed.

Matthias had been sizing up the carriage for about thirty minutes and was trying to stash his satchel somewhere inside the roof when Harry sprang around the corner.

"What?" said Matthias.

"The alarm, did you hear it? They must be bringing him here."

He looked around and listened. The sound of bells was very faint but he could hear it none the less.

"Thanks," he said. "You've done your part now. You don't need to stay."

Harry looked back with a face that said otherwise. "We're here for you. We'll stay out of sight though. This is *your* mission."

His friend turned to exit but ran into Gerard and Evan who had just walked around the corner. Gerard sneered and shoved Harry backwards and he fell to the floor.

"There you are," he snapped, "I knew you'd be up to no good!"

Matthias turned around from the carriage where he was preparing to hide, "What do you want Gerard?"

"Didn't you hear the alarm? You should be in the courtyard not sneaking around. Mr Cook put us in charge of rounding up the students. I knew you were up to something in here yesterday. Get away from that carriage!"

Sophie arrived behind the boys looking perplexed. Gerard noticed her and turned on her too.

"You stupid little girl," he said, "What are you doing with these two? Is one of them your love perhaps?"

Matthias made his way over and put himself between Gerard and Sophie.

"Go away," he said. "This isn't anything to do with you."

"Oh, it's you isn't it? Being all brave in front of your beloved Sophie."

Gerard shared an exaggerated laugh with Evan and then turned to look down the stables.

"Here come two of Mr Cook's men, Matthias. Let's see how you explain this one."

Matthias cursed Gerard; he was going to ruin everything! Perhaps he could reason with him? Offer him something to just go away. If the soldiers thought there was anything suspicious going on they were bound to investigate. A detailed examination of the carriage and they'd doubtless find him, unless Gerard betrayed him first.

But then a movement from the corner of his eye made him look across at Sophie who had suddenly gone pale. "Those aren't Mr Cook's men," she said.

"Of course they are, stupid," said Gerard, and turned to wave at them. "They're over here, sirs!" he shouted, pointing at Matthias.

Sophie started walking back to the carriage, "Gerard, don't!"

Evan stepped forward now, "We found them, should we report back to Mr Cook?"

The two men's faces were in shadow and they increased their pace as they turned into the enormous room. Matthias noted they were out of uniform, all wearing dark clothes with cloaks.

"You're for it now, Matthias," said Gerard, with delight in his eyes. He turned once more to look at the approaching men who were now only yards away. Evan was walking to meet them and as he did so they drew their swords.

"Gerard, get back!" roared Matthias.

"What are you doing?" said Gerard, but he would never get an answer.

It all seemed to happen so quickly for everyone else but Matthias saw it as if time was moving at a snail's pace. The man closest to Evan stepped toward him and pulled his blade back high. Matthias again called out; but with no time to react, or even move, Evan just looked puzzled. The man struck the boy with a slashing blow across his head and he crumpled to the floor dead before he reached it. Everyone froze and watched as the men drew closer. Harry appeared from nowhere and grabbed Sophie, pulling her back to the carriage.

Matthias followed and when they reached it all three spun just in time to see the other man withdraw his sword from Gerard's chest. The poor lad managed to look at Matthias and mouth for help as he too, fell where he stood.

The man wiped his rapier on his boot and then turned to confront the three by the coach. The other stood blocking the entrance of the chamber but made no move towards them. Now Mathias realised what was happening – these soldiers were preparing an ambush of their own. They must be Nunez's men!

The closest looked up and as he did Matthias caught sight of short black hair and dark eyes. The man paused and looked to the other for some instruction. The taller man by the doorway, who was dark-skinned and with a shaven head, nodded and then gestured to the three friends or at least it should have been three - Harry had taken to the shadows!

Excellent, thought Matthias, as he drew his knife; that would give them something to think about. He looked to his right and could see Sophie pull out her own knife and start to reach inside one of the pouches she had around her waist.

He spoke to her, but kept his eyes on the advancing man. "I'll stand my ground. You get behind the carriage and do what you can."

Sophie gazed back, her face pale. She blinked, lost in the moment, before nodding and retreating behind the coach.

The man approached Matthias and made to attack. When it came it was slow and off target. A feint, Matthias realised as he stepped back with ease – the man was seeking to judge the boy's ability. Another swipe followed and again he stepped back. This time the man chuckled and his vile laughter echoed around the stables.

The man pressed forward again and Matthias stepped sideways this time to avoid being backed up against the carriage. *Where was Harry?*

Another, more serious lunge, followed. Matthias stepped to the side and brought his knife crashing down on the foil. From his training he knew where the sweet spot was and the blade clattered away causing the man to hold his wrist in pain. Snarling, he stepped back and pulled out his own knife and then attacked again; this time reaching out with his arm as made to grab Matthias.

He held his ground and ducked the attack slipping around the man's waist and bringing his blade upwards as he did. The edge of the knife scraped at the man's flailing arm and he cursed. His tough leather clothing took most of the blow and he turned to face Matthias again. The man swung once more and again Matthias was too quick; but as he stepped back he found himself pressed up against the wall.

The man stood in front of him and breathed heavily. Matthias was cornered and he looked around for Harry but saw nothing. Then, suddenly, there was a voice. It was Sophie screaming, "Close your eyes!"

Neither Matthias nor the man really knew what was coming but it was Matthias who came off the least worst as the flash bomb hit the wall above them; Partly due to him facing away from the wall, and partly to at the last second remembering what Sophie had in the pouch he'd seen her reach for.

With the buzzing still in his ears he slowly regained his sight and saw the man crumpled before him. His eyes were staring blankly at the floor and his hands were over his ears.

Still groggy, Matthias rushed past him to reach the stagecoach and Sophie, but she wasn't there. He turned and scanned around the back but again he couldn't see her. Then his heart sank as he looked to the door and saw the other taller man with the shaved head holding a knife to her throat. He was standing in the shadow of some barrels and with his other hand he brought his finger up to his lips instructing Matthias to be silent. He nodded to a pile of boxes in the corner.

Sophie's eyes pleaded with Matthias but it seemed they were out of options. He duly walked to the shadows of the boxes in the other corner of the room. As he got there he felt a crushing of his chest as the other man appeared from nowhere to grab him and restrain him with his knife.

"So it was you in the forest last night," he hissed in Matthias's ear.

The figures from the trees – it had been Nunez's men! If he had known he could have raised the alarm – why had he not investigated? As Matthias cursed himself the man pulled him in tighter and held a knife to the base of his skull.

To the left of him he saw something move by the carriage; it was Harry, knife in hand lying underneath the coach. He caught Matthias's eye and nodded; as Matthias shook his head in response the man pushed the knife harder against his neck. Harry clenched his fist but the two boys realised situation was hopeless.

Then, they waited. It seemed like hours but was only minutes. Voices, footsteps and then the familiar figure of Mr Cook and his guards but with a prisoner in tow. It was Balthazar Nunez. Matthias squirmed under the grip of the man holding him as he looked into the face of the murderer.

He was unshaven and his long black straggly hair was unkempt and dangling across his face. He was bloody and bruised – perhaps the work of Alonso? His body was lean and strong looking but his face gave away the evil depths of his nature.

Matthias instantly knew this was the man he had seen at the abbey. He knew this was the man he had to kill. But now he was about to get away and possibly he would lose his own life too. His shoulders sagged in the grip of the man holding him. He almost felt like asking him to get it over with.

As the soldiers entered the room it was Mr Cook who realised something was not quite right. Maybe it was the smell of the flash powder? He paused and looked around. Matthias wanted to scream out but knew it would mean quick deaths for him and Sophie.

Then Mr Cook knelt down and touched the floor. He had spotted blood on the spot where Gerard had fallen. With a sickening realisation Matthias saw that the bodies of Gerard and Evan had been moved on to the floor only a few feet away from him. The man holding Sophie must have moved the corpses in expectation of Mr Cook's arrival.

Before Mr Cook could even draw his sword the man had stepped from the shadows with Sophie in his arms, the knife still placed against her throat. Then, it was Matthias's turn. His captor dragged him into the dim light of the room also and there the men remained showing their ransoms to Mr Cook.

"Weapons down," said the man holding Sophie. "Or I kill her."

From the corner of his eye Matthias saw Nunez, held between two soldiers, dangling limply from their arms, suddenly lift his head. He sensed freedom.

Mr Cook looked around the room trying to size up the situation, one hand still on his un-drawn sword. Calculations made, he nodded slowly and then ordered his men to place their swords on the floor.

Lastly he drew his foil and laid it carefully on the cobbles.

The man holding Sophie stepped forward and Matthias was dragged closer too. The two men now stood side by side facing Mr Cook and his soldiers, each holding a hostage.

"Release him," said the man holding Sophie. Mr Cook looked at Nunez who was smiling then nodded to one of the soldiers who stepped forward with some keys to release the prisoner from his irons.

At first, Nunez fell weakly to the floor. Then he got to one knee, breathed deeply and finally stood up. He started to massage his wrists and looked at the soldiers with disdain.

"Mr Cook," he said in a coarse whisper, "it's been a pleasure. But regrettably I must be on my way. I believe I saw the gates had already been opened? Gentlemen."

He started to make his way to the door and as he did so both his men shuffled sideways around Mr Cook and the soldiers; keeping their knives pressed against Matthias and Sophie's throats.

As they reached the exit to the chamber Nunez spoke once more, this time to Matthias and Sophie.

"Thank you, children, you've been most kind," He nodded to his men who released their grips on the two before throwing them to the floor. The men turned to flee as Mr Cook and his men quickly reached for their swords to chase.

Matthias could contain himself no longer and shouted, "My name is Matthias Cortés!"

Nunez looked like he'd walked into a wall and his companions only noticed after they were half way down the corridor. He turned around and faced Matthias who was now flanked by Mr Cook and his soldiers.

"Matthias?" he said, arching his eyebrows. "I have so wanted to meet you." He licked his lips.

"That's correct Balthazar," said Mr Cook. "Looks like you missed your opportunity. Care to try again?" He extended his sword in front of him and the soldiers did the same, holding a tight formation around the children.

Balthazar Nunez smiled and his cold blue eyes shone through the dim light. "Not today, Mr Cook," he said, "not today." He turned and fled with his men whilst the others remained.

Mr Cook turned to Matthias. "Take Harry and Sophie and fetch Mr Hardy and Alonso. Tell him we've set out after Nunez."

Matthias was still glaring at the dark figure shrinking into the distance and rounding the corner of the stables entrance.

"Matthias! Do as I say!" Mr Cook and his men set off, swords in hand, after Nunez.

Harry grabbed Matthias and they made their way to the doors at the other end, although with each step Matthias fought harder and harder to go the other way.

"He's getting away!"

Harry shook his head, "No, Mr Cook will catch him." They reached the door leading out to the back of the stables near the kitchens and rushed out straight into someone.

"What's happening?" It was Alonso; his enormous arms stretched either side of him to prevent the children from passing.

Sophie, Harry and Matthias all started to drown him with information at once. He looked at them sternly after picking through the pieces. "Where are they now?"

"Mr Cook followed them out of the castle gates," replied Sophie.

"We haven't much time, come Matthias," said the mystic.

"What?" said Sophie.

"You two return to Mr Hardy and deliver your message. Matthias, we can take horses and cut off Nunez."

Sophie looked to Harry for support, her eyes wide. "You're taking Matthias?"

The Spanish mystic looked down at Sophie. "It is his destiny. I have seen it."

Chapter 19

The mystic whipped the horses into a gallop sending them both back into the seat. After a few minutes silence Alonso turned to regard Matthias and once more the boy felt his very soul being examined.

"What unfolded back at the castle was unfortunate," shouted Alonso, above the noise. Since the mystic had rushed him onto a carriage before speeding out of the castle gates Matthias had hardly had time to think about what had happened. '*Unfortunate*' was an understatement. They had seen Mr Cook and his men disappear into the distance on horseback, chasing Balthazar and his men who had taken steeds from the stables.

"The two boys," Alonso continued, "they should never have been in the stables. From what I can tell your plan was sound and you may have succeeded. It would have been quite right for your first kill to be Balthazar Nunez. After all, he murdered your sister."

"You see killing and murdering as two different things," said Matthias, shielding his eyes against the wind.

"Of course," said the mystic, "Why else would there be two words in your language?"

He let the thought roll around his head. Was there a distinction? The carriage leapt up to the left as the wheels kicked off a large tree root at the side of the track. The castle was shrinking into the distance now.

"To kill a man may be necessary; to defend yourself or a loved one perhaps? In the midst of a battle or for revenge...Murder is something quite different."

"How can we find him?" asked Matthias.

The mystic tapped his head. "I know where this man goes. I see his path."

"Am I to kill him?"

"You cannot deny your destiny, Matthias. This man must die by your hands. I spared his life when I captured him. I knew he was meant for you. *This* I have seen."

Ahead of them the trees loomed over the road stretching out and creating a canopy. Within seconds they were engulfed in a dark green light. Matthias looked ahead, his eyes searching for signs of Mr Cook or Nunez. There was none and the road looked undisturbed. In the hot summer heat the surface was dry and hard so it would be difficult to spot tracks.

He turned back to Alonso. "You, I mean your people, see things don't they?"

Alonso smiled and turned his attention back to the murky road ahead, "Yes."

They started to ride alongside a stream. Its waters trickled busily away behind them, the light bouncing off the tops of the ripples like crystal.

"We see what may come to pass. It is never complete and often more like looking into a deep fog. But sometimes you see pictures. Hear voices. Or feel an emotion."

Matthias nodded, "Like when you remember something? Except in reverse?"

Alonso smiled and gave a chuckle. "Yes, that is exactly it. In all my years I have never heard it described so but Matthias I think you have, as you English say, *hit the nail on the head*."

"But what do you see of me? What do you hear? What do you feel?"

Alonso slowed the horses down to a trot. They were breathless but still had plenty to give. He had to pull them in hard to keep their eager legs from mounting a surge.

As they slackened the wind hushed and the carriage wheels slipped into a slow trundle which bounced around the branches of the trees. Alonso turned to Matthias and said, "I see a great destiny. I see blood. I hear your laughter. I hear your screams. "

Matthias sat back and steadied his gaze on the road. "How does it make you feel?" he whispered, in truth not really wishing to know the answer.

"Frightened," said Alonso.

They had continued for about thirty minutes when up ahead they saw a figure lying in the road. Alonso spoke softly to the horses as he slowed them down and the creatures came to a standstill a little way from the body.

"Stay here," said Alonso. He lowered himself off the carriage and gently stepped down. Around them was tall grass and on the right side a lonely oak created a shadow over the road.

The Spaniard took out a long knife and cautiously made his way forward to what looked like one of Mr Cook's men. Arriving at the body he bent down and touched the man's neck, his own knife still in his hand.

"His throat has been slit."

"From behind?" said Matthias, remembering how this could be told from a physiology lesson.

"Yes, it means they were ambushed, this was no swordfight." The mystic continued past the body looking all the time downwards. About ten yards further he bent down and touched some dust before looking across at the oak tree.

He beckoned Matthias to join him and the boy leapt down, but made sure his landing was soft. As he approached, he was aware of every whisper from the breeze snaking through the long grass and every groan from the branches above.

Alonso looked at him, but his eye seemed to be focused behind the carriage. "We are not alone; stay with me. When they make their move stand fast, but do not attack unless they do so first. Do you understand?"

Matthias nodded. "Mr Cook?"

"I do not know," said the mystic, getting up. "There was a struggle here in the road and at least one body was dragged off behind that oak. No doubt they have seen me checking the tracks. It won't be long now."

He followed Alonso back to the carriage, each step seeming to last longer. When they reached it Alonso gave him a hand up but didn't step up himself. Matthias watched as the mystic started to adjust some of the straps on one of the horses.

"What are you doing?" he asked, leaning over the side.

"The bushes over my right shoulder, can you see them?"

"Yes."

"Is there still a man lying in the grass?"

Matthias felt his chest pulsate and looked. "No, I- wait!"

He could see a man beneath the thicket, lying down in the long grass, about twenty yards away. He didn't let his eyes dwell for fear of giving away his advantage. Looking back at Alonso, he hid his fear with a nonchalant shrug. "Yes, I see him."

"Good. There is another behind the carriage making his way closer. I fear they do not intend to take prisoners. Are you ready?"

"What do I do?"

"Underneath the seat is a loaded pistol. Shoot the man behind me and I will make my way to the back of the carriage to greet our friend." The mystic ducked between the horses to get around the back of the carriage.

"Wait," hissed Matthias, his eyes kept looking around for movement. "I'm a terrible shot!"

Alonso looked down at his belt, pulled out his knife and started back the other way. "Now would be a very good time to correct this."

Matthias looked down at his feet and could just make out the hilt of a sabre and next to it the handle of a pistol; the flint sticking out from under the seat. It wasn't cocked, so he'd have to do this before aiming. Under normal circumstances, on a calm day stood in front of a target, he struggled with a pistol; this wasn't even close.

When he looked back to Alonso the mystic was gone. He had only seconds to act; any time now Alonso would be at the back of the carriage taking on the other man. He looked up again, judged the distance, picked a spot in the grass to focus on and then reached for the gun.

His hands shook for a second as he pulled it out from underneath the seat. The stock felt warm and soft in his hand. He cocked it, still hidden from view, before taking a deep breath and raising it at the figure in the grass. As he did so the leaves shuffled and he saw the head raise, a dark silhouette against the green and yellow blades. Then he fired.

The figure's head rocked back unnaturally and fell.

For a second he stared at the grass, the pistol still held out in front of him a thin wisp of smoke circling out of the barrel. Then his senses returned. The smell of the gunpowder, the brightness of the sky and the scream of a man behind the carriage.

He leapt to the back of the roof and looked over only to see Alonso pulling his blade from the neck of one of the men from the stable. The mystic discarded the body with a shrug before putting his finger to his lips and edging around the side of the carriage.

He followed him from above and then saw what the Spaniard had seen. Nunez was standing in the middle of the road, alone. "Excellent, Matthias. Bravo. I can assure you the second one is much easier," he said.

Matthias grabbed the sabre from under the seat and leapt down onto the dirt. He was ten yards away, the shade of the branches etched across his features. The sun was low, arresting his silhouette from behind.

He inhaled rapidly, his face staring intently at Nunez. Then, just as he lurched forward, his shoulders reeling, an arm grabbed him and pulled him back with such force his feet momentarily left the ground. He spun around snarling, but it was Alonso.

"Wait," said the mystic.

Matthias's teeth were bared under his lip and he snorted.

"Quite right," said Nunez. "As I'm sure Alonso suspects I do have another card to play."

From beneath his cloak Nunez produced two pistols. Both barrels faced at Matthias. Less than ten yards away it was unlikely Nunez would miss even if he could rush him.

"How did it feel to kill your first man?"

"Not as good as it's going to feel killing you, Nunez. I will avenge Rebecca…and all the others."

"She was an abomination," hissed Nunez, "as are *you*. I don't know what you've been told Matthias, but their blood is not on my hands."

"How so? You were the one who butchered them like animals."

Nunez gestured toward Matthias with one of the pistols. The man's scraggly black hair was blown back from his face by the breeze and he looked at Matthias with revulsion.

"What you are is an insult to everything we fight for. What was done was done to be certain, no more. Sadly, it looked like you slipped through my fingers. But today young *child of the fountain* you will die."

Matthias didn't understand these last words but knew from the man's body that he intended to shoot. So be it, he thought. If he shoots and hits me, at least Alonso will kill him.

It was almost as if the mystic read his mind for no sooner had Matthias thought this than Alonso was stood beside him, holding his long and bloody knife.

"No Nunez," said Matthias. "Today you will die and then the rest of the Legion when Alonso finds them.

Nunez cackled and shook his head. "The Legion are not a force of evil, we are a force for good; cleansing the earth."

He felt his left hand go down to the pouch at the back of his belt. Felt his fingers touch the soft paper inside. Felt the flash bomb in his palm.

"Don't be afraid to die, Matthias."

He looked Nunez dead in the face. "I'm not afraid to die. You already took my world from me when you killed my sister."

Nunez scoffed, the pistols dipped slightly toward the floor and he opened his mouth to speak, but then a noise made him stop. It was the unmistakeable sound of a rifle cocking.

Nunez didn't move; his eyes rolled wildly around in his sockets as he desperately sought the source of the noise. But he couldn't see behind him, where Alexander stood, a rifle held tight under his chin.

"Alexander?" said Matthias, "What are you doing here?"

The older boy spoke, but never took his eyes off Nunez. "I saw you leave the castle in a hurry Matthias and thought you might need some help." There were tears in his eyes but he managed a weak smile. Was he scared?

Alonso stepped toward Nunez, "Drop your pistols."

Nunez stood, still as a statue. "I could still kill you Matthias. Tell your friend to drop his gun."

"If you kill that boy I swear I will murder every last Nunez on the face of this earth!" screamed Alexander.

"That boy?" A pause, Nunez searched for air. "Michael?"

The young lad pulled back his shoulders. "It's Alexander now. Michael's still in here though, somewhere."

Alonso straightened, Matthias turned to look at him but even the Spaniard had not seen this.

"When you killed Margaret," said Alexander, "it took every ounce of my strength not to come looking for you. It was my father who persuaded me to wait. You were too strong back then, the Legion's forces were everywhere. So I went back to the fountain."

Alexander calmly paced around to the side of Nunez; the rifle was now inches from the man's temple. "I came back, of course, to protect Matthias and Rebecca. But you killed her too."

Nunez was still staring; he wavered ever so slightly on the spot. Then, he jolted, and remembering he had the pistols brought them up, still trained on Matthias.

"When Alonso caught you I was promised justice. But then you escaped. I followed and watched you ambush William who, by the way, is safely tied to a tree behind me. Alonso, would you be so good as to release him?"

The mystic nodded and disappeared into the grass. Making his way toward the oak he was soon lost from view.

Matthias looked at Alexander, the awkward shy boy from the castle. Gone were the innocent, bright eyes. The soft lips were turned into a snarl and he could see, though somehow he'd never noticed, that every muscle and tendon was toned and strong like a wolf. So this is what had happened to Michael Cortés; he'd been hiding in plain sight all along.

"Whatever I do Michael, you're going to kill me anyway. So why should I not take the boy with me? Complete my vengeance."

"Vengeance? You dare to speak of it?"

"I watched my wife die! Your fool of a father could have saved her." Nunez's eyes opened. "One drink! That's all I wanted."

"My father guards the fountain to avoid such tragedies as this."

"Well, I don't think you can avoid this tragedy."

"That's what we're going to find out. You see Matthias is quick, just like Margaret."

Nunez stared at Matthias for a second; and in that second Matthias saw everything.

He saw Nunez reach a decision. Watched his fingers twitch on the pistols, glimpsed the sparks from the flint, the puff of smoke from the barrels and the jolt from Alexander as his own rifle fired as well.

But Matthias was already turning, diving to the ground, rolling backward and away from the shots he saw trail above him, inches from his face. When he landed on the floor he rolled over several times before stopping and, without thinking, sprung to his feet.

Nunez was lurching forward, blood across his head. He must have avoided Alexander's shot somehow as he was now lunging at Matthias; a crazed and hungry look in his eyes. Matthias's hand reached to his belt without thinking and he brought out his knife, leapt forward. Nunez's blood stained hands clawed at his face and he tasted the man's blood in his mouth.

Somehow he managed to grab his neck and with all his might thrust the dagger upward as the two rolled to the floor. They spun, Nunez on top and then Matthias before finally they lay side by side.

Balthazar Nunez looked confused momentarily, but then his eyes snapped wide open. Finally, comprehending what had happened, he opened his mouth but no noise came out. His eyes rolled into the back of his head as blood streamed out of the side of his throat.

What may have been a scream of pain was followed by convulsions. The body finally stopped jerking, and lay still at Matthias's side. He stood up and looked down at the man he had waited so long to kill. His eyes raced over every detail. The hair, the hands and feet. The clothes, the shoes all looked so normal. But the eyes. The eyes looked back at Matthias as if from Hell itself.

For a while he stared, unsure whether to know what to say or to even look at his father. But then he felt a soft hand on his shoulder and an embrace. It felt strange, hugging this boy who was barely older than him. But it also felt right, his father cried.

"My son. I'm so sorry."

Chapter 20

Matthias looked across at his father from inside the coach. The sun was high and cast shadows down either side of the roof. Through the open window he could hear the horses snorting and the wheels thundering slowly over the road.

"This must seem strange for you," said Michael Cortés.

Matthias stared blankly at the boy only a foot away, their knees jarring together every time the coach went over a rock. "What should I call you?"

"For now, it must be Alexander."

Time rattled on. The coach wheels kept turning. He wasn't sure if it was for minutes or hours that he looked out of the carriage window. Alexander, his blond hair catching the sun and illuminating his head, merely sat and waited.

Alonso was sat above driving the carriage; Mr Cook sat next to him nursing a bruised head. The mystic had suggested they have time alone to talk. Nunez's body was on the roof in a sack; Alonso had stated it should be returned to his family. Matthias had been in too much shock to even think about it, but now that he did he felt revulsion knowing the corpse was only inches away.

"You must have a lot of questions," said Alexander, shifting forward in his seat. "When you are ready I will answer them."

"Questions?" said Matthias, and let the word hang in the air. Alexander shifted in his seat. "I lost my home, my family. I was taken into a life that I feel I'm still only able to grasp."

Alexander nodded. "I can only imagine how you feel. It has been quite a change."

"Quite a change?" he leaned forward now, his lips peeling back from his teeth. "I was trained to kill. Shown how to use weapons and learnt every part of a man's body that I might end his life. I chose a future of war, assassination and revenge. I bathed in it. Nurtured every sweet moment of hate I felt toward the man who murdered my sister and then finally killed him. And now, my father steps forward out of the shadows. Feel? I feel nothing, sir. I have no feelings left."

Alexander nodded slowly. "You have your mother's temperament."

Matthias scoffed and shook his head. Another minute went by and he too stared out of the window at the passing countryside. He didn't know what to say, yet he wanted to say so much. Why couldn't he talk?

His heartbeats started to slow down; he thought of Rebecca. What would she have done? She would have been more frightened than him, but a father – the one thing she had always yearned for. If she had been here, Matthias would have taken the lead. Consoled her and questioned their father on her behalf. Eventually, he decided he would try to understand.

"What was my mother like?" he said.

"The most beautiful woman in the world and one of the most intelligent," said Alexander, as he sat back, his gaze lost in memory.

"What happened to you?" said Matthias.

"After your mother died I too wanted revenge. But first I had to hide you and your sister. James agreed to take you in; though our father didn't give him much choice."

"Does he know about you?" said Matthias. "I saw you in his quarters. I thought perhaps you were helping out in the chapel."

Alexander smiled, weakly. "Your uncle understands I lost my faith a long time ago. But in answer to your question, yes, he knows who I really am. It was quite a shock when I told him. You know about the fountain?"

"Yes, he explained what happened; your father and the others."

"After I had hid you and your sister my options were limited. The Guard was weak back then; it was shortly before the war and our numbers had been depleted in Europe. That's when I came back to the castle and met Father Morant."

"The monk who had been writing all the histories."

"Yes. James tells me you have read some of them."

"Bits. He was teaching me to read. It was the family trees that helped me piece things together."

"But the histories were just part of what he had been writing about. You see, Morant was really a man of science; something that sat at odds with the church. When he was taken on as chaplain for the castle he delved in to understanding the nature of the fountain and all the gifts it had bestowed on the children; either through direct contact or breeding.

"He told me of his theories and it was through these teachings I designed my plan to go back to the place where it had all began. Ten years it took me. I sailed across to the Americas and with little more than a scribbled map and a few legends I found it; but only after the jungle nearly killed me.

"It was still there. So perfect, so beautiful. The fountain was already in my blood so to drink from it? Well, I didn't exactly know what was going to happen. When I drank, everything changed. I became younger, but my mind remained the same. It took several days, at times it was quite painful. But eventually my body transformed into who you see before you now. My younger self.

"I made my way back and holed up at the castle. The plan was to speak to you and your sister when you were old enough. Nunez changed all that."

Alexander clenched his hands together then settled them on his lap. "Did she suffer?"

Again, for a moment, Matthias was back at the abbey; amongst the screams and blood. His friends' faces flashed past him, always just at the side of his vision. They were crying out to him, pleading. But Rebecca somehow looked peaceful. Her death had been brutal, but quick.

"No, she did not suffer."

"If I'd have known I would have never left you both."

"What now?"

"I must remain as Alexander. The Legion will doubtless pursue the loss of Nunez. It could mean another war."

Matthias allowed their eyes to meet. "Will you stay at the castle?"

"Perhaps, for the moment. It was Lady Taylor who led the men into the castle, she has disappeared however."

"I saw her in the forest, last night," said Matthias, "but I didn't realise she had betrayed us."

"Lady Taylor pledged her service to the Guard a long time ago. Do not be so quick to judge her in attempting to save her brother's life, even if it was a wicked one. I'm sure there was nothing you wouldn't have done for Rebecca?"

Matthias nodded. Alexander continued, "Alonso and I have some unfinished business to attend to."

"You two are close?"

"Alonso and I go back a long way. It was my proximity which clouded his visions of you. He saw two lives touched by the fountain, entwined in a past, present and future."

"His prophecy?"

"My transformation caused certain ripples in his mind. I think he mistook those ripples for a sign; a sign that led him to you."

Above them he heard no sound from the mystic, but both felt his presence. It was almost a feeling in the air you couldn't quite perceive. But there was also an impression that he was able to hear every word you said.

"You must finish your training," said Alexander, "if you are to be ready."

"Ready for what?" said Matthias.

"Whatever comes next."

Chapter 21

The journey back to the castle proved, thankfully, uneventful. When they arrived it was dark and Alonso urged Matthias to get some rest as Mr Hardy would doubtless want to see them in the morning. Alexander said he had to return to his dormitory, lest he be missed.

"I'll speak to you soon," he said, placing a hand on Matthias's shoulder.

He nodded and watched as his father, the man he thought dead but who was alive and trapped in the body of a young man, disappeared through a castle door.

He turned to Alonso, "Did you know?"

"No, his future is empty. Perhaps the fountain has changed his soul; certainly his body. But his mind is still very powerful."

"He said I needed to be ready for whatever happens next. What do you think he meant?"

"A war, perhaps," said the mystic, who was now climbing up to the back of the carriage to retrieve the body. He did so with ease and threw Nunez's corpse onto the floor. He beckoned over a student who came to help.

"Vasco Nunez will want to avenge his son's death, no doubt." The mystic looked down at Matthias, the solitary eye gazing far beyond the boy. "I could always say I killed him?"

"No," said Matthias. "It was me. I want him to know who did it and why."

"Help me with this," he said to the student, a young boy who had no idea what it was. "I must go now, your father wishes to talk to me alone."

The mystic gave him a friendly smile and then he and the boy walked off around the back of the castle, carrying Balthazar Nunez with them.

Matthias headed inside. Making his way through the corridors of the castle he was sure the other students who saw him regarded him differently, several moving aside and trying not to make eye contact. Word couldn't have gotten around that quickly? But then he realised he had blood on his clothes.

As he neared the chapel he started to feel anxious about seeing his uncle. Knowing how the monk felt about killing he was unsure of what reception he would receive. Guilt and nerves ran through him but it all washed away when he saw the old man turn from prayer at the altar and hold out his arms. The embrace felt good.

"Matthias, it's so good to see you return safe!"

His uncle was happy, but there was also concern hidden in the depth of his eyes. "Mr Hardy told me you left with Alonso. Let's go to my study, I have some food."

They made their way to the back of the chapel and along the corridor. As usual, the small room was stacked high with writing and the single candle projected the shadows of piles of books onto the wall making them feel like they were surrounded by enormous buildings.

"I hear Alexander helped out," said James, almost casually.

"You mean my father?"

His uncle paused, holding an apple just above the fruit bowl for a moment, before turning and offering it to him.

"He told you?"

He nodded and took a bite. The monk sighed and leant back on his chair. "I was wondering when he would."

"How long have you known?"

"The day I arrived; I saw him in the corridors." Father James chuckled, "He looks just like he did when we were younger. At the time I gave it no further thought; when you have lived as long as I have the memory plays tricks. But he visited me that night and every day after."

"That day I came in?"

"Yes, he had come to see me and when he heard voices quickly pretended to clean the floors. He's never so much as lifted a scrubbing brush in his life! I knew I couldn't lie to him and had to introduce you as my nephew."

"That's why he acted so strange."

"Indeed, for a second I thought he might let his secret out. But we both knew it was too dangerous. We had to work out what to do with you."

"I've been doing fine on my own."

"Your bravery is to your credit; but you lack experience."

"We have so much to catch up on; I want him to teach me."

"I can teach you too." The old man sat down and ran his fingers through what little of his hair remained.

"You must understand," he continued, "To them this is all a game. A deadly one but a game none the less; one I chose to have no part in. Perhaps they see in you a replacement for me." He sighed, "If only my father would end this futile war."

"But what of the secret he guards?"

"It is God's secret Matthias. We should have faith he will see fit to exercise his plan when he chooses."

They talked until it was late. Father James shared stories about Matthias's father, they both recollected about the abbey. Finally, he felt his eyelids draping downwards.

His uncle offered him some hot milk before he left, which he gladly accepted. Afterwards he made his way back to the dormitory where the sounds of Harry's snoring could be heard even from outside his chamber. Getting into his bed he drifted off with gentle thoughts of his uncle, glad that he had some connection to hold onto in his rapidly changing world and for the first time in a long time he slept peacefully.

At sunrise he ate with his friends in the mustering hall. Both Harry and Sophie were desperate to get all the details they could out of him.

Harry's jaw almost hit the table when Matthias told how he'd picked off one of Nunez's men with a pistol and it was Sophie's turn when he spoke of killing Balthazar himself.

"Are you okay?" she asked.

"I'm fine."

"How did it feel?" asked Sophie.

Matthias looked back at his friend, her face showed no expression. "I feel happy, I think," he finally said.

She nodded, "Yes, I believe you do."

Before they could get any more detail out of him a student arrived to tell them they were ordered to go to Mr Hardy's room. When they entered he was playing with his moustache and reading a letter on his desk. He pointed to some seats across the room, "Sit down, all of you."

The master looked at Matthias, Harry and Sophie from behind his desk blankly. The fire crackled and spat from one corner and the only other sound was the great clock that looked on from the shelf behind his chair. As it ticked away each second with its ancient mechanism, time seemed to slow down. Indeed, Matthias could feel the pause between each 'tick' and 'tock' get longer.

Finally, Mr Hardy looked straight at him and spoke, "What you did was extremely foolish."

Matthias looked at the floor unable to meet the man's gaze. Harry and Sophie followed suit staring at their shoes or some crack in the stones.

"Because of your actions two boys are dead."

Harry's head shot up at this, "We tried to warn them!"

"Dead!" bellowed Mr Hardy. Harry breathed in and sat back as if he had been delivered a blow.

"The man who we *suspected* responsible for the massacre at the abbey almost got free, but was then killed; taking any intelligence he may have had with him and I have two dead children on my hands. Is any of this registering?"

Silence descended on the room once more when Mr Hardy paused, but he was not finished. "I have to write to their parents, Matthias. Have you any ideas on what I should say? 'Killed in the line of duty' perhaps? An 'accident' during training?"

Matthias swallowed hard and finally brought himself to meet Mr Hardy's gaze. The master was still sat behind the desk, his palms facing down onto the oak.

"I don't know, sir," said Matthias.

"Maybe I should just tell the truth? That they died because of the wanton revenge of a boy? A boy who wished to take the life of the man who destroyed his.

"A boy who needlessly got his friends involved in a botched assassination and whose actions enabled a murderer to almost go free and in doing so endanger the lives of everyone in this castle. A boy whose sheer arrogance meant that their sons ended up caught in the crossfire. Do you think this is what I should write in the letters?"

"It was a trap. Nunez's men were already there. If it hadn't of been Gerard and Evan it could have been someone else."

"Yes, Matthias. It could have been anyone else. Or, Mr Cook could have dealt with them as he had intended to after receiving word from his spies; that is why he came to the castle – he knew of the plan. But we will never know if Mr Cook would have succeeded as when he did arrive they conveniently had hostages."

The crushing weight of Mr Hardy's statement made him wobble on his chair. His head rolled back and he stared at the ceiling and closed his eyes. What had he done? What price had he paid?

Gerard was a bully and Evan a weasel, but they hadn't deserved this. If only he could go back. If only he could change it. But he couldn't and now he had the blood of two more people on his hands; only these were innocent.

"I didn't know," he said, his voice croaking.

"No, you didn't. We have rules, Matthias. I'm sure you know them by now. I won't patronise you by pointing out why you should have obeyed them. We live in a very dark world; our code is our only source of light."

Mr Hardy turned his steely gaze to Sophie and Harry. "As for you two, you should have known better."

"Yes, sir," they both muttered.

"I trust all three of you wish to continue your training here?"

They all shared a glance and nodded. "Your punishment will be three months of extra duties. Harry, I believe you already have a role in the stables, Sophie will assist in the kitchens and Matthias you will be working in the chapel.

"With regards to yesterday's events I'm sure you understand the need for discretion and so will ask that none of you to speak of this again, even to each other. Am I *absolutely* clear on this?"

All three nodded. Mr Hardy got up and reached for his coat and some papers, "Harry, Sophie; come with me to the records office, we have some paperwork. Matthias, please remain here."

He stood and nodded as they made to leave before he was left alone with nothing but the sound of the clock to keep him company.

Minutes passed, images whirled in his head as he digested what Mr Hardy had just said. The guilt settled down in his stomach like a weight; and it wasn't going anywhere. He kept telling himself it wasn't his fault, but it sounded like another voice in his head – pretending. Although then another voice spoke, *Nunez is dead! What price wouldn't you have paid?*

Would he have let them die if he had known? His hands felt the arms of the chair he sat on. He looked down and saw warped, yellow wood where the varnish had worn. How many other sets of hands had clawed at these arms? How many other students had sat here in Mr Hardy's office and pondered their fate?

There was no getting over a part of him didn't want to turn back the clock. Gerard and Evan were, ultimately, a price he had been willing to pay. The Legion had declared war on him; there were going to be casualties he would see to that. They must be stopped and here, at the castle, was the best place for him to help with the fight.

Harry and Sophie were his friends now and the thought of something like what happened at the abbey happening to them filled him with rage. Here, the children were trained. They were killers. *Let the Legion come*, he reasoned.

Chapter 22

Mr Hardy had still not returned when the clock struck the hour. Matthias was thinking about getting up and leaving when the door swung open and in strode a powerful looking man with a full moustache and fine clothes. A cape swished open revealing a sword and he held the door open behind him. Matthias shot up not knowing whether to greet the man or prepare for a fight.

The gentleman didn't acknowledge him but scanned Mr Hardy's office; although what he was looking for Matthias couldn't fathom. When the man seemed satisfied, he stood aside, his back to the wall. The sound of quick, bold footsteps was shortly followed by an old gentleman with a neatly trimmed white beard and mischievous eyes underneath a fine black hat.

He sat down on one of the chairs next to Matthias and dusted himself off before speaking to the man at the door. "Thank you, Doyle," he said, taking off his gloves. "You may leave us."

The man at the door nodded and left the room shutting it behind him although from the lack of footsteps Matthias could tell he was still stood outside. He turned his attention to the man sat beside him. He wore pale blue breeches with a matching waistcoat, his shirt was silk with delicate cuffs. On his fingers were several rings; all gold and adorned with precious stones. Finally, around his neck, a thick gold chain with an amulet Matthias couldn't quite study hanging about his chest. The eyes were pale blue and mischievous; he'd seen them before or a pair very like them. Two pair, in fact.

"You're my grandfather," said Matthias.

The duke regarded him with a grin, "Very astute." He paused and looked around, inspecting every corner of Mr Hardy's office as if reacquainting himself with an old friend. "Well, isn't this nice?" he said, finally.

Matthias opened his mouth but no words came out. He simply had so many questions and things to say he felt he would make no sense if he did. Slowly, he sat himself down but continued to stare.

"You must have a lot of questions?" said the old man, leaning over to Mr Hardy's desk and pouring some water. As the drink churned to the top of the cup the duke glanced over and raised an eyebrow, "Well?" he said. His voice was croaky, but sharp.

Something about his posture suggested that underneath the clothes his body was not so frail as the white whiskers implied.

"Well what?" said Matthias.

"Well what do you want to ask me?" said the duke, looking visibly irritated. His voice was firm, with a slight accent similar to Alonso's, and he was clearly surprised at not being understood.

"Why?" said Matthias, after some time. "Why am I here? Why is Rebecca dead?"

"Good questions," said the duke, sipping from his goblet. "Are you a religious boy, Matthias?"

"I go to church. Father James teaches me as well."

"Ah yes, James. How is he?" The duke drained the last of his water and placed the cup carefully back on the desk.

"He is well. Have you not seen him?"

"Oh, I'm sure he's told you we don't get on. You see, Matthias, I am not a spiritual person like my son. I find it difficult to attribute acts we see to that of a divine entity. Until he reveals himself to me I choose not to follow James's *God*."

"You have no faith?" said Matthias.

"I have seen too much of the world and for far too long to know that if there is a God, he is not the least bit interested in how we choose to pass our years living and dying. So no, I have no faith in God.

"You're looking at me and your eyes tell me you pity me. Please, save such sentiments for those who truly need them. Piety I tolerate, but righteousness I do not."

Matthias had never asked himself how he felt about God, the same God that had allowed the carnage at the abbey. Perhaps he was a believer; or perhaps he went to mass every Sunday just to spend time with his uncle. "I have always had the church in my life," he stated.

"Man created the church. Not God. Did God tell us to gather every Sunday in a big cold room and mumble our thanks to him in an ancient language? Your uncle would have us believe so."

"This is because of Vasco?"

The duke's eyes widened, "You're quick. How much did he tell you?"

"He told me about the fountain. About the children. About me."

"You're very special, Matthias." The duke leant over and held out his hand, "I would very much like you to take this hand and tell me you want to help end this evil war. That you will help me keep the fountain from the hands of those who would use it to carry out evil deeds in the name of their Lord. I want you to tell me your sister did not die in vain."

In vain? The old man was trying to make her death sound noble. The fury rising up inside him was quelled only by the fact that this man was his grandfather and a connection to the family had he never had. Every inch of him wanted to cry out in rage but equally, he just wanted to sit and stare at the man.

But the fight, the fight against the Legion, that was all he had now. Dark days were ahead but hopefully, the darkest were behind him. Yes, he would take his hand. And yes, he would take up the fight. For his revenge grew ever hungry. Nunez had not been enough.

"I will."

The white whiskers parted and the duke smiled, slowly. "Good."

"What now then?" Matthias asked.

"You will finish your training. I hear you are doing rather well."

"Well enough. I excel at some things more than others."

"When the time is right I shall call for you, but you still have much to learn. Pay attention to your tutors, read the books." The duke tapped his temple with his finger.

"What of my friends? Will they come with me?"

"If you wish," said the duke, standing and gathering his coat. "You seem to operate well as a team. But remember, for us, friendships are temporary. Family is permanent."

Matthias stood up too. "What do you mean? Harry and Sophie *are* my family now."

"Sophie? Ah yes, I believe she is a descendant of my good friend Alonso de Ojeda. Her story is quite sad." A flash of concern crossed his face and he absent-mindedly stroked his chin.

"As I said, you are special. Both your parents are direct descendants so the fountain's water is in your blood. In fifty years' time you may still have the body of a young man. Both your friends will be old, maybe even dead by then. Slowly as you drift through life you might have to come to terms with your own immortality."

"We don't die?" said Matthias.

"Not yet," said the duke, with a smile. "'Although, as they say, *mors vincit omnia*."

Matthias blinked and stared at the duke. The old man's face leaned in closer and he kissed Matthias on the cheek, "Death always wins."

He walked to the door and opened it before turning around to face Matthias.

"Until the next time, Matthias Cortés, I bid you farewell. Good luck with your training. I shall, of course, be taking a very special interest in your studies."

"What about my father?"

The old man turned to the cold corridor, the draft running through his hair like fingers. "He will be coming with me to London. We have much work ahead of us and my son is…reinvigorated."

With those parting words he left. His guard closed the door behind him and Matthias heard his footsteps echo away down the corridor.

Chapter 23

It was a cold frost which arrived quickly that November. It seemed that one week they were enjoying the last throes of autumn underneath copper-leafed trees, and the next they were fighting their way to lessons through blizzards and snow.

But still they continued. Still they trained. Matthias felt himself getting stronger as all around him suffered and fought the depths of winter. It was the pain. Somehow he thrived on it and found himself looking forward to long runs, target practice in the rain or bruises from sword fights.

Harry and Sophie noticed this change in Matthias as he became more focused and dedicated. He soaked up the knowledge and skills on offer before retreating to his room to study or re-read books. They both said he seemed to spend more and more time alone. The closeness that the three enjoyed seemed to be disappearing and they began to drift their separate ways. True, their classes kept them apart as they specialised in their own subjects, but it was something more. Harry even suggested that Matthias was avoiding them.

Christmas arrived without much change. Some of the other children went home. Matthias and Harry who had no family stayed and, to both their surprise, so did Sophie. It was on Christmas Eve when lessons had officially finished for a week that the two concerned friends managed to sit down and have him all to themselves.

Alone in the mustering hall, Matthias was immersed in a volume on fencing he had sought out in the library. One hand was holding the book and the other an imaginary sword as he tried to replicate the moves he was reading about. Harry, never one to miss an opportunity for a joke, leapt in front of Matthias's mock blade and feigned a mortal wound.

"Argh! I'm done for!" he exclaimed, dropping to the ground in a heap. His smiling face was met with a frown from Matthias as he rose. Sophie sat down and Harry joined them on the table.

"We've been worried about you," she said. "How are you keeping?"

He sighed and closed his book. His eyes were tired and he rubbed the bridge of his nose and yawned.

"Tired," he said. "But I really want to make sure I complete my apprenticeship. O'Grady's got me working harder than ever and biology still confuses me."

"We don't see you anymore," said Harry. "You're either out training or in the library. You're never there when I fall asleep and when I wake your bed is made and you've already eaten. Is everything alright?"

He thought for a moment. He was only too aware that he had been pushing himself but not realised how isolated he had become.

"You're right," he admitted. "It'll be Christmas soon. We should make arrangements to celebrate together."

"Matthias," said Sophie, "Christmas Day is tomorrow."

He looked a little surprised. "But I thought today was the twentieth?" Sophie and Harry shook their heads. "Maybe I have been pushing myself. But I have to."

The two friends again looked at each other for guidance. It was Sophie who offered some solace. "You don't need to prove yourself, Matthias. You killed him."

"But I failed *her*," he said. "If I could have done then what I can do now…"

"You weren't ready," said Harry.

"I let her down."

"You can't blame yourself," said Sophie.

As Matthias looked into the eyes of his two friends something became apparent. He knew that as long as Harry and Sophie stayed at his side it didn't matter what trials came his way. Rebecca was gone, but in his place were a brother and sister whom he knew meant nearly as much.

He smiled. "Come on," he said, "let's go and find something to eat. Maybe a bit of supper in the kitchens? They'll be pretty quiet now."

Harry leapt to his feet. "Now you're talking," he said, with a grin. "Let me just go and get out of my field gear." He slapped his friend on the back and headed off to their dormitory to get out of his thick leather jerkin.

Matthias started to pack away his books. Sophie yawned and turned to face the fire warming her hands.

"Sophie," said Matthias. She didn't turn around but responded with a sound of recognition, "My grandfather, he mentioned something about you."

"Really?"

"He said your story was a sad one."

He could hear her slow breathing. She kept her back to him; sat across the table staring, he assumed, into the fire.

"A lot of our stories are sad, Matthias. That's why we're here."

He wasn't sure whether to press, but out of concern for his friend's pain he asked. "Was it to do with your parents? They're dead aren't they? That's why you're here for Christmas?"

"Yes, they're both dead. They were murdered, in fact."

"I'm sorry to hear that," said Matthias. "I didn't realise. Was it the work of the Legion?"

Sophie chuckled. "Good Lord, no!" she said, turning around with a strange smirk on her face. Matthias returned her smile but he wasn't quite sure why.

"It was me," she said.

Epilogue

As Vasco Nunez emerged onto the deck a crisp wind sprayed his face with salt water. *The Americas*. He was almost there, but he felt no pleasure in returning. Over the bow of the ship he could see a green crescent of land sitting below the horizon, the sun's rays hitting the fields and trees, before reflecting off the ocean.

He looked around as the ship's crew busied themselves for their arrival. She was a fine vessel, one of Mr Greene's best. *It was such a shame about him; it would have been useful to have kept him. A large shipping company, plenty of ties to the Americas. No matter, Mrs Greene could handle the reigns, it just might eat into the time of her other commitments.* As a sailor made his way past, Nunez calmly took the man's arm and pulled him close.

"How long till we arrive?" he whispered. The seasoned sailor was taken aback and struggled politely from the man's grip.

"We'll be docking at noon, signor," he said.

Nunez nodded and let the man go; then slowly he walked to the bow and leaned over a rail so he could gaze at the churning white waves. Vasco Nunez was an elderly man, unshaven, but immaculately dressed. His hair was a light brown, tinged with white streaks. His mouth, downturned and sour, was closed in a frown.

After some time a figure appeared behind him. A shorter, plump man, dressed in dark red velvet. His eyes were shielded by a round hat, but the unmistakable crucifix catching the light around his neck marked him as a man of the cloth.

"Cardinal," said Nunez, "I trust you rested well?"

"Well enough," said the cardinal. His voice was high pitched but soothing and he breathed in deeply the sea air. "We have much to prepare. I trust you have made suitable arrangements for our journey?"

"Yes, we should be underway tomorrow at noon. We'll spend no more than a day in Rio before we set off. However, I am not comfortable with our choice of allies."

"We both have a vested interest in the events that may or may not unfold. I ask you to work *with* them, but you do not have to trust them."

Nunez scoffed and turned his attention back to the horizon. "What of my other task?" he said, raising his voice over the crashing sea. "My son found the boy."

The cardinal sighed and looked down at the deck. "Your sacrifice has been greatly appreciated," he said, "but you have to understand some believe he went too far."

"You were aware of his methods."

The cardinal came to stand next to Nunez and he too gazed at the ocean. The luscious green land of the Americas was beckoning him and his hand crept across his chest to touch the crucifix. He brought it to his lips before, bowing his head, he spoke softly.

"Yes, I was aware of his methods. Alas, my superiors do not share the same understanding of God's work as you and I. The boy will have to be dealt with soon enough but, for now, we have our tasks. From what we understand, when we return in two or maybe even three years he will still be just a boy."

Nunez scoffed, "Just a boy. Indeed!"

Sailors unfurled rigging and the ship started to lurch towards the port side. "You see him as a threat, don't you?" said the cardinal.

Nunez tilted his head to one side. "Maybe," he said.

"Why?"

"Because when I was his age I had already killed ten men," said Nunez. "Matthias Cortés does not even know how truly dangerous he is."

The End

Acknowledgements

The online self-publishing community has been a vast source of information, tips and guidelines. To all those people out there writing, blogging or even just chatting in the forums – I salute you.

I'd like to thank David Robson for his fantastic original artwork. It was stirring to see the characters I created brought to life on canvas.

I'd also like to praise David Mitchell for his design work and lettering. His creativity added that final professional touch.

In advance, I'd like to thank all my friends who I know will be tweeting, 'liking' and sharing the book on my behalf. I hope everyone enjoys it.

Finally to my wonderful wife Helen who has been an inspiring source of strength in everything I do and whose help made completing this book possible.

For more information please visit:
www.richardpmurphy.com

Printed in Great Britain
by Amazon.co.uk, Ltd.,
Marston Gate.